V.O.I.D.

Victory Over Instant Disappointments

Barbra JuDon

iUniverse®

V.O.I.D.
VICTORY OVER INSTANT DISAPPOINTMENTS

iUniverse books may be ordered through booksellers or by contacting:

iUniverse
1663 Liberty Drive
Bloomington, IN 47403
www.iuniverse.com
844-349-9409

Because of the dynamic nature of the Internet, any web addresses or links contained in this book may have changed since publication and may no longer be valid. The views expressed in this work are solely those of the author and do not necessarily reflect the views of the publisher, and the publisher hereby disclaims any responsibility for them.

Any people depicted in stock imagery provided by Getty Images are models, and such images are being used for illustrative purposes only.
Certain stock imagery © Getty Images.

ISBN: 978-1-5320-7615-2 (sc)
ISBN: 978-1-5320-7616-9 (e)

Print information available on the last page.

iUniverse rev. date: 09/15/2020

FOREWORD

It is not my objective to burden you with the when, where, what and how of Creation as if within my human limitation I could ever comprehend this phenomenon with certainty and clarity. However, I'd like to speak to the Why?

The question is why would our God take the time to create humanity? What purpose do we serve? Were we really needed here? I'm sure I'm not the only person that ever questioned our existence.

It seems as if not only did God create humanity but I certainly believe we are the greatest of His creation simply because we were according to Genesis chapter 1:26-27, made in His image then given the charge to rule over the Earth that was prepared and awaited our arrival.

It is my belief the Lord created humanity simply for His pleasure, and it is this reason we should love Him, Worship Him and make Him the center of our lives.

And with this truth in mind, God insured communion with Him by creating man with something missing. A VOID if you will that was designed to be filled only by Him. No money, no career, no home, no car, no jobs, no relationships or people were never a replacement. It is that part the VOID within us that belongs only to God.

Pastor Nah-tarsha Cherry

ACKNOWLEDGEMENTS

First, I want to give praise to God for pouring
into me the words to put on these pages.

Special thanks to Pastor Nah-tarsha Cherry for her
unconditional love, patience and mostly her timeless
efforts to make sure this book was correct.

Thanks to all my family and friends for they continuous
encouragement. I love you all for the bottom of my heart.

BJ

There is about to be an earthquake in Beverly Jensen's young life, not the kind that breaks up the ground and destroys buildings, but this earthquake is of a different kind. This is the kind that breaks down a person's self-esteem and makes them feel lost and confused.

It's a sad time right now in the lives of Beverly and her dad. One evening while they were watching TV and just when Beverly was coming to grips with the fact that she did not have a mommy and determined to be okay with that, she heard a loud crackle of thunder.

A storm was brewing outside, but something else was brewing inside. This would be Beverly's stronghold, her disconnected puzzle pieces that haunted her for many years.

The phone rang, and her dad went to answer it. Before he hung the phone up, he called "baby girl come here," they both heard the person on the other end say dead. That was all Beverly remembers hearing the words SHE-IS-DEAD!! "DEAD."

At that precise moment, Beverly was not sure who was dead, but her dad looked sad. He almost looked as if he wanted to cry, he was quiet and in deep thought. Beverly *thought wow, that phone call made Dad sad.* Then he said, "Beverly, Ms. Delores is dead."

Beverly was not sure what dead meant, but she knew it upset her dad. Ms. Delores was the same woman who while in the bathroom washing Beverly's back one evening, told Beverly "I'm not your mother." Those stuck in little Beverly's young mind all her life.

"Dad, what does dead mean?" He said, "we would not see her anymore." So, Beverly's next question was, "Daddy is my mommy dead too?"

Why didn't Daddy ever answer Beverly's question? Did he not know the answer or was it a secret? We all know adults keep too many secrets.

That is the reason why Beverly could never forget this night. The night Ms. Delores died.

The next few days were busy ones, her father told his daughter they were going to a funeral, she thought to herself, *why do they have to go?* A typical question for a nine-year-old right? A few days later Beverly and her dad attended Ms. Delores' funeral.

A big black car was parked in front of our house and Beverly and her dad got in the back seat. Beverly remembered how gloomy the day was.

After the funeral as they drove past the house again, Beverly was thinking they were getting out, but instead they stayed in the car and went to where they put coffins in the ground. Oh, they called it a cemetery; it was a scary place at least that was how it made her feel and what was worse it was cold and raining.

The next event was like someone threw an extra-large ball at Beverly that scattered her thoughts. They were in the back seat of this big black car, and these disturbing words came out of Beverly's Dad's mouth pierced Beverly's small heart.

It was a rainy day in November, Beverly could not remember what year exactly, but what she remembered was that day was the worse day of her life.

Beverly's dad said, "Beverly you will not be living with me anymore. You are going to stay with Uncle Shorty and Aunt Naomi." She started crying because in Beverly's young mind she just knew she had to take care of her dad because they needed each other.

Not understanding this situation, when they got back home Beverly ran into her room and cried her eyes out until she fell asleep.

The only thing she heard in her young mind was her father saying she would not be living with him anymore.

The next months were estranged between Beverly and her dad. He seemed to talk less and drink more. When school ended in June Beverly's dad packed her stuff and they left together.

Beverly cried and said, Daddy please don't make me leave I'll be good, daddy please. Beverly an only child didn't understand WHY?

Her dad said, "baby girl you have to go." That day she was separated from the only parent she'd known. Beverly couldn't imagine what she had done so bad that her dad didn't want her anymore. She never got a spanking or even yelled at for anything. So, in her innocent mind she was feeling confused and sad.

She moved from upper Manhattan, Washington Heights to a place called Harlem. Beverly never knew there were so many other people that resembled her living in one place. Her old block had a mixture of white people, some Irish and Greek, Cuban and another Colored family.

Shortly, after moving in with Uncle Shorty and Aunt Naomi, Beverly overheard a conversation between the two about her dad. She overheard them saying he was admitted to the hospital several times, but Beverly did not understand why he was so sick.

Beverly heard them saying he was in some part of the hospital that locks people in their rooms. She was not allowed go to the hospital to see him because she was too young.

Nobody thought that she needed to see HER dad.

Beverly's life was like a puzzle some pieces fit and other pieces were lost forever.

Beverly needed to see her dad; *he needed her she reasoned in her mind. Why did he leave her with these people?* Beverly always asked herself this question. Besides that, Aunt Naomi was always yelling, something Beverly was not used to. They had a daughter named Lori who lived downstairs with her son, and she was not very friendly either. Beverly went from a quiet house with just her and her dad to a dysfunctional loveless home. Now she's with a family full of mean people and this would change Beverly's outlook on life, especially from a young girl's perspective. Her life had gone from happy to sad.

The bedroom they gave Beverly was small, so she would sit on the fire escape at night trying to stay cool in the summer. She watched kids play games like softball and kickball until it got dark outside when everyone went home. Beverly missed playing with her friends on her old block. She was not very happy here, not at all.

Beverly constantly thought about her dad, looking forward to the day he'd be coming back telling her *"let's go home baby girl."* She heard him say those words in her dreams, but so far that had not happened, however, she held on to hope.

Beverly also knew there was a cousin named Henrietta that her father had introduced her to that worked in a beauty salon. He dad took her there before dropping her off at Uncle Shorty's house.

Cousin Henrietta told Beverly that she could make some pocket change if she wanted to come to the salon in the afternoon's and Saturdays.

Beverly was excited to hear that so every chance she got Beverly would walk from 135th Street to 125th Street every morning or early afternoons and on Saturdays to her cousin's beauty shop where she got paid to run errands and clean the shop.

Beverly often worried if her dad was taking care of himself? But the emptiness she felt always caused a flood of tears to stream down her face. She was torn between love and anger for her father. In anger she questioned how could her Father think this was a good idea leaving her in this house with these strangers.

She questioned herself every time she had to look at Uncle Shorty's face, why me? Why did he touch her private parts? and forcing her to sit on his lap while he unzipped his pants? Beverly felt helpless, dirty, lost and confused and all these emotions were overwhelming her. She thought about running away, but that scared her because if she did not find her dad where would she stay.

So, years later Beverly played hooky from school and decided that it was time to find her way uptown in search of her dad. She went to their old building but her first stop was the corner bar. This was the place she always found her dad when she came home from school.

She walked in and looked around for familiar faces. Ernie the bartender was still there. She asked him had he seen her dad because everyone knew him. They all said no, but they knew he had been in the hospital and that was the last time they heard about him. One of the men told her, "I went to visit him, but the hospital informed me that your dad could not have any visitors."

Later, Beverly found out that her dad had been in the Psychiatric Ward. It was not until years later that she would understand the effect of the disease called alcoholism.

Beverly really did not know her dad had a serious drinking problem. After hours of searching for her dad, she was tired. She decided to visit the only other Colored family on her old block, praying they were still there.

The Wilsons were the neighbors down the block and were overjoyed to see her and invited her inside. They asked where she was staying, and she felt she could confide in them. So, she began telling her story and by the end of the evening, Beverly cried harder than she had in a long time. She was a little girl that felt unloved and unwanted.

They offered her to stay with them for the weekend and Beverly did not think twice about it. She asked if she could call her uncle. Uncle Shorty just said, that was fine with them, so everyone sat and enjoyed a great meal that evening. The Wilsons thought it was best that Beverly should stay with them, but Beverly said, she just wanted to find her dad.

Therefore, the next day Beverly, Mary the Wilson's 15-year-old daughter and Natalie, Bev's best friend promised to help Bev look for her dad.

By that evening they had no luck and Beverly flopped down on the sofa speechless. Beverly had told them almost everything except the part about Uncle Shorty. She did not think they would believe her story anyway, and she felt too ashamed to tell anyone.

The Uncle that made her sit on his lap also, made her promise not to tell anyone. Beverly remembered the nasty feeling she felt when he told her to get up. Those demons would lay dormant until whenever.

Beverly did stay the weekend still hoping to run into anyone that might have seen her dad, she refused to give up her search. The Wilsons allowed Beverly to stay with them for the summer or longer if needed. This was a good solution for Beverly because Uncle Shorty wanted to take a trip and they had not planned to take Beverly anyway. Beverly overheard them talking one evening about the trip and she knew they did not want her there anymore so at least she would have a good summer. After that, she did not think about the hurt uncle Shorty caused her.

The next day Mr. Wilson drove Beverly, Mary, and Natalie back downtown; they walked upstairs into the apartment Beverly spoke then went and packed her clothes, Mr. Wilson told them, she is leaving because she found her dad. Mr. Wilson knew exactly who Uncle Shorty was. And Uncle Shorty didn't object to what he had just been told. Yes, it was a lie, but he never tried to stop Beverly or object to the fact that she was leaving.

Filling a Void.

The summer had begun, and the girls spent their days having fun, just as Beverly remembered. On Sundays the girls would walk to the movie theater. As they were leaving the movie theater on this particular Sunday they look up and suddenly there he was Beverly's father walking down the block.

Another earth-shattering event is about to happen in Beverly's life again. He looked way smaller than Beverly remembered, he was tall but very skinny now. Nevertheless, that was him, her dad. Beverly ran toward him and hugged him so long he had to pull her away.

Beverly was so happy to see him again. "Hi, baby girl, look at you, looking all grown-up!"

She was almost twelve years old and it had been 3 1/2 years since they'd last seen each other. The girls were excited for Beverly too. "Oh my gosh!" the girls shouted we found him!

Beverly started asking her dad questions. "Dad, how are you? and where have you been? And why didn't you come back for me?"

"Wow, slow down baby girl," he said, "come on Dad lets go to the Wilson's place you remember them?" Beverly grabbed her dad's hand she was excited and happy.

He went back with them to the Wilsons place they had been friends for a long time. Her dad did not look well, but Beverly didn't notice that now.

Mrs. Wilson offered him dinner and they all sat down to eat just like old times.

"Beverly how's Shorty been treating you, good?" Immediately tears ran down her cheeks. "Beverly, what is the matter?" She choked up and the only thing she could say to him was she's never going back to that house again, never dad... Beverly could not say any more and the next thing she heard was her dad telling her she was going with him. So, she gathered her things, hugged the Wilsons and the girls, said her goodbye's and left with her dad.

Beverly's stay with the Wilson's was cut short. Dad thanked them for letting her stay, but he said she could not stay with them. While traveling on the train she asked her father was she going to live with him? She wanted to stay with her daddy. Her dad said, "unfortunately, baby girl you will not be staying with me."

Beverly's little heart sunk. He continued explaining to his daughter that he had been sick, and only had a room a few blocks from where they lived before. He also told her he'd been in the hospital several times, not ever saying exactly why, and she did not ask either. All she wanted to do was stay with him. She put her arm in his and fell asleep during the ride.

Filling A VOID

When they exited the train station, Beverly questioned where they were and he explained to her that they were in the Bronx.

Beverly asked him after they arrived, isn't this my cousin's house, she remembered visiting them several times. They were her cousins, but she always called them Mom and Pop as long as she could remember. Another drop off for Beverly.

Before her dad left again, she asked him would he come back and get her soon. He smiled and said, "let's see what happens, baby girl."

After that day, Beverly never saw her dad again. The day Beverly had dreamed about, the day her dad would come and get her never happened.

It had been two and a half years and nothing from dad. Not a phone call or a visit absolutely nothing. She was happy that Mom and Pop treated her as if she were their own child. Beverly felt loved and cared for because she was connected to a family again.

Beverly and her three cousins had chores, rules, and strict discipline that Pop would tell us every week this would develop them into strong adults, and as a reward, they could go to the movies on Saturday afternoons.

School was difficult for Beverly and she never really connected with it. It was hard because she never stayed in one school for any length of time. After about a year of hearing nothing from her father, Beverly would stop crying every night and hoped that he did not forget his only daughter altogether.

Being at Mom and Pop's house was the best thing that had happened to Beverly. She was hoping that this would be her permanent residence. Her second family, people that actually loved her.

Mom would tell Bev every day, how much she loved her, and took her shopping which became a whole other level of fun. She took her to stores like Bloomingdales, Macy's and Sak's Fifth Avenue. This was the reason when Beverly got older, she loved shopping in boutiques for her clothes.

Beverly confided in her cousin about her dad and that's when Beverly came to the realization that she might never see him again. Mom expressed her concern for how Beverly felt and said she loved her no matter what her father did or didn't do. Beverly believed she would stay with Mom and Pop forever.

Beverly seemed to fit right in with her cousins. Mom treated her just like her daughter, in fact, she called Beverly her daughter instead of her cousin. Mom also had two sons and a daughter, whom Beverly called her sister and brothers, instead of her cousins. Beverly remembered saying to herself, *"finally I belong to someone."*

But this wouldn't last long when one day her cousin informed her that she would be leaving again! Immediately shock, hurt and disbelief flooded over her and sadness filled her days again. Another move? Why? Were they tired of her? she wondered. Beverly thought, *would she ever get what she wanted which was a family, her dad, and love.*

Beverly always thought *that she was the worse kid on earth because nobody wanted her for too long.*

Beverly's next move was with Mom's sister that had just moved from Harlem to a house in the Bronx. The same cousin Henrietta that worked in the beauty parlor (that's what they were called years ago), the owner allowed Beverly to work with her as the errand girl. She'd been working there for a couple of months, well until she moved with Mom and Pop. Beverly missed her little spending money.

Henrietta had two sons; Beverly thought they were the two smartest guys Beverly knew except for her other three cousins. Beverly thought they were close to geniuses.

Their dad was smart too he knew about so many different topics and discussed interesting subjects. They would have debates about different issues and Beverly would be amazed at all the details discussed daily.

Prior to living with them, Beverly had not been exposed to all this knowledge. Her older cousin Trav would help Beverly with her homework on a level she could understand.

Now like her sister Henrietta also took Beverly shopping and bought her nice clothes. By this time Beverly was hurting, angry and feeling wothless and she became very promiscuous during this time just wanting to be loved, trying to fill a **VOID**.

There was another move brewing because they were moving to Mount Vernon this time she was included. But she couldn't help but wonder *for how long this time?*

Beverly was excited about the move because she would have her own room again and would make new friends. Once Beverly started at the new school she could not keep up with her studies and she failed almost every subject.

So, after the last year at the Junior High School and her first year of Mount Vernon High School, it was decided to move Beverly back to the Bronx to finish school there. Beverly felt she was an embarrassment to the family.

Now she was moving with Mom's daughter Arlene another cousin and her son. Arlene owned her own restaurant in the Bronx. By this time, she disliked school and her life, but every day she took her cousin's little son to school; Beverly loved this kid. He was smart like her other cousin's sons.

Beverly was always searching for something, she felt hopeless. So, she decided to find a job, because the school thing wasn't working for her, so she became a high school dropout, she needed money and she needed a plan.

Beverly left school and got her first job in a warehouse. She made friends, maybe not the best ones but at least they were there. They partied, drank, smoked and just hung out, something most young people did.

Eventually all this partying led to Beverly wanting her own place. She had to come up with a plan to pay rent and still be able to party, because she was tired of moving around.

She felt she could make it herself, if she worked. Beverly was smart and lied about her age to get jobs and at fifteen Beverly was working at a warehouse.

Beverly saved up her money a little every paycheck until she had enough to move into an apartment There were apartments as cheap as $350 monthly. Unfortunately, Beverly couldn't find a halfway decent apartment anywhere.

Beverly always felt lost and depressed and never really sure what her outcome would be, but she was determined to succeed no matter what happened.

One day Beverly coming home from work ran into a friend of Arlene's named Phyllis who lived with Arlene and Beverly for a time. Beverly and Phyllis had become friends although Phyllis was much older than Beverly they would go shopping together sometimes.

Eventually, after hanging out a few times Phyllis invited Beverly to stay at her place until she found an apartment and be roommates. It sounded like a good idea to her she would finally be independent and on her own.

Yes, she agreed to move into Phyllis' place, not knowing she only had one bedroom. Beverly was all right with it because she was working and planned to go back to school. Her plans didn't fall into place until years later.

Phyllis suggested that Beverly work where she worked because they needed a waitress. Beverly had been a waitress just months before in Arlene's restaurant and became good at waitressing, but what Beverly didn't know was that Phyllis worked at a nightclub and bar.

For Beverly to work there, Phyllis lied and told Joe the owner of the bar Beverly was older than she really was saying she was almost 20 years old and he hired her immediately. Beverly knew nothing about working in a bar, but Phyllis showed her the ropes. For the most part, the money was decent, and she made good tips too.

Beverly had to grow up quickly all her young life so now she really felt grown–up. The work was steady, and Beverly was a quick learner, so before she knew it, she was behind the bar mixing drinks and flirting with the men that came in and out of the bar; it went with the territory.

The bar would become Beverly's evening and weekend job. She still worked at Marlene's restaurant during the week.

Months later Beverly learned about a program where she could learn to type since the bar was not really what she wanted to do long-term.

Beverly's tenacity was pushing her in a different direction, and she knew that she needed a stable job with benefits. Beverly even bought a typewriter to practice making sure she passed the entrance exam.

After three attempts, she finally passed the test and began taking classes. Beverly was a dropout working two jobs but after those classes she had a skill that would pay off years later.

Working at both the restaurant and the bar kept money in her pocket, but somehow her roommate never had any money. Beverly started wondering why, she was always claiming to be broke. She worked longer hours than Beverly did, so why? What Bev hadn't realized was Phyllis had two habits, a drug problem and a gambling problem. This was causing friction between them mainly because Beverly needed to save money to get her own place to stay.

It became difficult to bring her friend's home when her roommate was fighting with her boyfriends. This situation caused Beverly to buy more food, and more household items because she never wanted to see her roommate hungry. Beverly also paid most of the bills that Phyllis was supposed to be responsible for, but again she had helped Bev out of a tight spot. So, Beverly felt it was only fair to help her out.

Working in the bar allowed Beverly to meet men of different ethnic backgrounds and different ages. They all tipped her well for serving them drinks and food whenever they ordered.

Beverly waited tables and remembered most of the customers names and their orders and never got them mixed up either. Thanks to a good memory, Bev had fun working at the bar. She loved to dance, and she danced with the customers once her shift was over.

One evening this gorgeous tall dark and handsome black man came to the bar dressed in an army coat. Bev's friends told her, if you meet a man in the service, your life would be good, you will get to travel and live a comfortable life.

So, there he was, she smiled and walked up to him asking him, "What are you drinking handsome?" He smiled back, and before she knew what happened, they were boyfriend and girlfriend. Her first boyfriend.

A year later they had a beautiful Christmas gift "A baby girl." Beverly was a mommy, but unfortunately, daddy had disappeared.

Beverly was on her own working and raising her daughter. She was seventeen years old and a mommy.

Phyllis and Beverly friendship came to a head on a snowy day after a terrible argument. The real reason Phyllis put Beverly and her baby out in a snowstorm was because Phyllis's boyfriend did not like crying babies. That was the last straw as far as Beverly was concerned.

So, she stayed at Karen's another friend who lived upstairs for the next few days. Then reluctantly she had to return to Phyllis's place. Karen had met Beverly's boyfriend and knew he was Beverly's daughter's father, so Karen convinced Beverly to let her get in touch with him.

About two weeks later, her daughter's father showed up and asked her to move to Brooklyn with him. Beverly was desperate to leave Phyllis's because it was always a struggle now that she had a baby and she also knew she could not stay with Karen much longer either.

Brooklyn was a different experience than any other place she had lived. Brooklyn is a great city and the neighbors were friendly folks, which made Beverly feel like she was on the block she grew up on.

Melvin was Beverly's daughter's great-grandfather and he loved his great-granddaughter. He shopped for the baby and supplied everything they needed. Her dad did not supply anything but a bunch of lies.

Beverly's daughter's great- grandfather told her everything his grandson had told her was a lie. He had never been in the army or any military and he did not even have a job. Beverly felt like a fool.

Beverly and her daughter's father argued constantly and soon Beverly had to decide whether she was going to stay there fighting with him or was she going to move out. Beverly was determined to take care of her child with or without his help.

Before she told him, she was leaving to move back to the Bronx, he told her his mother Ms. Eva was willing to help in any way she could.

Beverly had never met his mother, so her willingness to ask for her help was not an option at this time. Beverly was angry and hurt, angry that she had allowed this man to fool her into believing he was something that he wasn't. Beverly explained since he had lied and continued to lie, she could not depend on him, so it was better that she left.

They had a child, and she wanted him to do his part in caring for her and he admitted that he had lied, but he would try to do better. Which was ANOTHER LIE!!

Beverly just looked at him because she did not believe him and would never again believe him. They were both young, but somebody had to be responsible and she knew it would have to be her.

Beverly packed up all her things and what she couldn't take she left. She contacted her cousin she called Mom and she made the arrangements for Beverly to move in with Beverly's cousin Arlene again. Beverly was a young single Mother, determined to try and be a responsible parent, whatever that looked like.

Since she never had a role model to follow, she hoped she could do this job correctly because parenting was a full-time job and didn't come with a manual. Beverly took her lead from what she had already experienced or at least that's what she thought.

After relocating back to the Bronx, the first thing Beverly did was find a job and a babysitter. Her daughter's father had reminded her again that his Mother was willing to help her.

This was Eva's first grandchild, and she was excited to see the baby. Beverly was still so angry with her daughter's father which made her put a block in front of her mind that told her not to trust anyone again.

After a couple of years of struggling, Beverly decided that she would take Ms. Eva up on her offer. The first meeting with "Ms. Eva" was an odd one, but she was honest and promised to help Beverly anyway she could.

Ms. Eva, as she was lovingly called, was clear on two things she was a beer drinker, but she worked, and she would not hurt her grandchild.

Beverly sat with tears in her eyes because she never wanted to leave her baby girl, but she had to work to provide security for them both. Ms. Eva apologized for her son, but she said to Bev, "You look like a smart young woman so try to forgive him I know it hurts, I've been where you are, but I had to make it without the help of his father too."

"You can do this, and Bev believe me you will." That was encouraging to Beverly. Beverly never forgot those words. Beverly felt that after their conversation she could trust Ms. Eva.

It wasn't easy to leave the baby, but she felt her child would be safe with Grandma Eva. They developed a bond; Beverly was able to discuss many of her problems and concerns with Ms. Eva.

Years later when Beverly graduated from college Ms. Eva expressed to Beverly how proud she was of her accomplishments. She said to Beverly, "I told you, you could do it". They both smiled.

Beverly felt Ms. Eva's love because she treated her as if she were her own daughter. Beverly hugged Ms. Eva and told her "I love you too Mama." Whenever she needed help, Beverly contacted Mama Eva, and was never turned down and she was always there to help just as she said from the beginning of their relationship. Beverly thanked God for Mama Eva.

Obstacles always come our way, but we must always strive to be better. Of course, Beverly, faced obstacles along the way trying to do things her way, trying to make moves, many times things did not work out.

Beverly tried to give her all to her daughter while still trying to find her own way. She stumbled countless times, but she got back up and tried it another way hoping to succeed. Many nights Beverly cried because she desired love and family and it seemed like that was never going to happen.

She finally realized she did have love, unconditional love from her beautiful baby girl and that thought enabled her to move forward with her life if not for herself at least for her daughter.

Through those years Beverly attempted to fill her **VOIDS** starting with partying, drinking, smoking and sex and with all that, she still felt empty. During this time things happened to Beverly that made her believe that only due to God's hand in her life did she survive.

Beverly had been molested by uncle Shorty for the entire time she lived in that house, years later she had been raped twice by some unknown assailants, a gun pointed at her head twice, thrown out and forced to sleep on a park bench, robbed, beat up, used and abused mentally and physically.

Beverly started keeping diaries and composition books to write down her feelings that she would not discuss with anyone - friends or family.

She wrote her feelings, her guilt, things she felt ashamed of, how abandoned she felt, and the distance from everything and everyone around her. You see Beverly had learned early in life how to put on a good act to hide her pain.

Beverly learned to adapt to her struggles and erase from her mind the pain, abuse or any other feelings that made her depressed. She would go dancing and forget all those stumbling blocks she faced in her young adult life.

That burning desire to have her own place was still eating at her and thanks to her typing skills she finally landed a job in a bank. She was working toward her first goal, her own place to call home. Months later her goal was met her first apartment was just around the corner from her cousin's Arlene's apartment.

By then Arlene had closed her restaurant, and this allowed Beverly to spend all her extra time with her daughter. She was beginning to appreciate motherhood differently now that she was living on her own.

Beverly kept her job at the bank because she promised herself never again would she be told to leave another person's home, she lost a few apartments, but she always found another one quickly.

Beverly's need to be accepted caused her to constantly choose the wrong kind of friends and men.

Trying to fill a **VOID**.

Beverly tried to be a good parent and care for her child the best she could and never wanted her daughter to feel unwanted like she had felt because her daughter's dad was not involved in her life. So, she tried to keep her daughter busy growing up.

She was a beautiful little girl, and they had good times and rough times, but they made it together. But as her daughter grew into a teenager somewhere in between the pain and trying to fill the **VOID** she lost her little girl.

So busy trying to fill her own **VOID'S**, she got involved with a man that within a few years showed that he did not love her, that he was incapable of caring about her and her child.

Beverly was drowning in her own misery so deep she could not hear her daughter crying for help because nobody heard Beverly's cries. This man that she thought loved her came between Beverly and her daughter in the worse way imaginable.

Molestation is a demon that attaches to vulnerable children and when we are broken, we draw brokenness to us, when we feel less than, less than lives, eats and sleeps with us. It will take our soul if we allow it too.

Beverly never wanted her daughter to experience the horrible things that she had and wanted most of all for her daughter to know her mother loved her with every beat of her heart.

She wrote a poem for her little Christmas gift. This poem was Beverly's way of saying she's sorry for not hearing her daughter's cries, not protecting her from the demons.

For being weak when she should have been stronger, wiser and smarter. When we lack love from a parent, we start forming walls of stone in our minds and our hearts. The lack of love and abandonment causes us to search for fulfillment. Unfortunately, not always in positive ways.

Molestation makes us victims and we become victims of circumstances that were out of our control. Men with their own baggage, their own issues seek like a missile to connect with broken women not all the time purposely to destroy whatever self-esteem they might have left. Because We All Still Need *LOVE*.

A Broken person can never heal another broken person. Only Jesus Christ can heal our brokenness.

We learn that the only way to become strong and re-believe in ourselves is when we surrender to the Lord, Our Savior. However, it was obvious Beverly had not reached that point in her confused messed up life yet.

Desperate to Fill a *VOID*.

IN BETWEEN

In between the attraction comes the love
In between the love comes the deception
In between the deception comes the babies
In between the babies comes the beauty
In between the abuse comes the pain
In between the pain comes the hurt
In between the hurt comes the years
Of trying to hope for better
In between the hoping comes the lies,
sorrow, mistrust, violence
In between it all, comes the end of
the fear, pain, tears, and lies
Then comes the courage to say goodbye
And in between it all she found Jesus

The enemy tried to separate her daughter from
her because Beverly did not know her precious
gift was hurting because she was hurting too.
But, through it all, her daughter never
lost her love for her Mother
"I Love you"

The Holy Spirit gave this to Beverly,
and she understood why.
Blessed be the Name of the Lord

Secrets that we as women keep to ourselves, sadly enough, can do more harm than good. Through Beverly's young life, she kept attracting negative men with their own demons into her life. Demons recognize other demons within.

Our low self-esteem causes us to make wrong choices for our lives. Some men and their demons can cause women pain and heartbreak. Many of us suffer from low self-esteem and low self-worth. Women have demons also, sometimes they are generational curses.

Everyone has strongholds and weaknesses; Beverly's was good-looking men, but she ignored their baggage. Their strongholds that they kept pent up inside without ever seeking help.

Beverly believed she was not a beautiful queen deep down, and her idea was if she pulled a cutie, people would envy her, saying, "How did she get him?" that was her low self-esteem talking.

Beverly's second encounter was worse than the first. This relationship produced twin sons: a peacemaker and a warrior. Beverly had, no idea that the turbulent relationship would leave her sons scarred for life. Two beautiful souls destroyed by a man they called Daddy.

The man that walked out of their lives when they were seven and never looked back. These two little boys that waited for their daddy to come by and pick them up, he would never show up again.

Abandonment had found its way back into Beverly's world again. On the other hand, had it ever left?

All Beverly could say is *"Help me, Lord."* Beverly had carried all those demons around in her suitcase for all those years; *molestation, abandonment, pain, mistrust, hurt.* For fifteen years, she stayed in this mess. The question was Why?

She believed it would get better every time. She didn't realize this was something he had done to all his previous woman. Beverly was not stupid, she was broken and needed God to rescue her from the mess she allowed herself to be in. God answers prayers.

One day he just up and left, she never asked why she just said, *"Thank you, Jesus."*

In the midst of all this confusion, Beverly graduated from The College of New Rochelle and was on the Dean's list too.

Beverly desired to prove to everyone and herself that she would not be a failure, she would amount to something, and she would not turn out like her Father or Mother whomever she was.

Sure, Dad walked out of Beverly's life then her daughter's father walked out of her life, then the twin's father walked out of their lives never looking back. Obviously, this was a pattern Beverly did not want to encounter ever again but she still attempted to fill a **VOID**, some years later.

One day Beverly met a handsome brother, he was sexy and cunning, **YES!** he fit the description that the enemy knew she would fall for again.

Along with this new relationship came new lessons. Beverly learned later that this handsome man was a drug user, liar, a thief and abused love. They started off great love flowed like a river, a beautiful relationship. Until his demons changed everything. While he was drug free, they traveled, they were in love and his family loved her. He never treated Beverly badly, but he treated himself badly.

His drug use got worse and he went in and out of rehabilitation programs. Many, Beverly helped him get into, but he kept making excuses for not completing them.

He always expressed, he did not want to lose her however, the truth was Beverly had become his enabler, something she found out years later through a promotion from foster care to the mental health division of her agency. As long as they were living like this, he was a nice, caring person.

Even with his drug problem, it was only once they married, did his hands find their way to her body in harmful ways. It was surprising to her because he never acted that way in the ten years that they were together, shacking up, as they say.

Beverly blamed his actions on the drugs, his "Alter Ego's" mind. She re-evaluated the situation, as she asked herself. *"Is this what God wants for me?"*

That's when she took her concerns to her Pastor, asking for counseling even though Beverly was a caseworker now helping people change their lives. We all need counseling especially if we have had a troubled life.

Pastor D.E. Wright, an anointed woman of God took the time to talk with Beverly and every day she enlightened Beverly on exactly how God wanted marriage and a husband to treat his wife. God's word is clear on this subject and His Word was new to Beverly. She was like a sponge eager to learn more about the Will of God for her life.

Finally, after her husband had gotten arrested the second time and got sentenced to four years, Beverly filed for a divorce. She was tired of the disappointments and the abuse that had followed her for so long. Beverly had been in a cocoon and was ready to break free.

She was desperate for some peace in her life. The peace that we can only receive once we decide to surrender our lives to the Lord.

This was the start of a new beginning for Beverly and it gave her a new outlook on life. God had saved her through His grace and mercy so many times, she could not even count them if she tried. Therefore, Beverly would never tell anyone that came from a dark past to give up on life. That darkness can turn to light once we open our hearts to receive Jesus Christ.

There will always be **VOIDS** in our lives, and they are there for many reasons, some we will never understand. God is the **VOID** filler. He is the Savior of our lives. He's the healer of our hearts. He's the provider of our needs.

There is no person, drug, money or anything that can fill the **VOIDS** the way God can.

Our **VOIDS** can become our Victories if only we trust and believe.

The Spirit of the Living God spoke to Beverly one day and said **V.O.I.D.** and she wrote it down. She did not understand why He would give her this word the way she wrote it.

Later it was revealed what those letters meant.

The **VOIDS** in Beverly's life were about to turn into Victories. The **VOIDS** that she kept trying to fill would never be filled by her own ideas.

No man, child, money, job, drugs, alcohol or sexual encounter would ever fill what God left empty for His purpose.

Beverly was about to walk into her victory. The voids of her past would become a mere shadow in comparison:

Victory Over Instant Disappointments

After Twenty-two long hard years working overtime, weekends, and holidays and after graduating college, losing friends, loved ones, boyfriends, and even a husband, Beverly had finally cracked that glass ceiling that so many Afro-American women tried so hard to achieve. Yes, it took sacrifice and lots of determination, but she was about to get her reward.

Beverly Jensen a divorced 48-year old woman, who had experienced a rough childhood was driven to become successful. Beverly is 5'4" dark-skinned woman with a beautiful smile that would light up a room, but when she was younger, men would tell her she had bedroom eyes.... It took her a while to catch on to that one!

Beverly has always been proud of her figure, so she works hard to keep it looking good. She is a person that people perceive as not being friendly, but once you get to know her, she has a heart of gold.

Beverly quickly moved up the ranks in position from clerk to supervisor, then manager and recently, well, not so recent she had been promoted to Assistant Executive Director, a position that she has held for the past 14 years and counting.

Beverly joined a prestigious Fortune 500 company 27 years ago. It has taken unbelievably long hours to get to this position, that she will be interviewing for in a few weeks. Beverly has a meeting with the C.E.O. and this interview is the one she's been praying and believing for that after 14 years in her current department, where the revenues tripled and its due time for her to shine in this company. Her first meeting is at 5 pm next Thursday and Beverly is aware that there is a Senior Executive position, which has been open for about a month.

Beverly will wake earlier than usual that Thursday morning, in anticipation of this important day. She stood in front of her closet to find just the right suit to impress the boss.

She decided on a gray suit with red accessories. Power colors! She smiled at herself admiring how she looked, she took about an hour in the mirror, and that was just to put on her makeup. She said to herself "Girl you're beautiful."

Beverly picked up her bag and headed to her blue Acura; she always liked cars that were classy. Her car was parked in the garage of her three-story eight-room townhouse. She remembered how she fell in love with this place the first time she saw it. The windows were from ceiling to floor with stained glass at the top of each. They reminded her of church windows and the doors were amazing, large stained-glass doors decorated with flowers and butterflies, (Bev had a personal connection with butterflies).

The house had high ceilings and beautiful wood floor plus, it had an enormous kitchen with so many cabinets that she lost count, there was a great seating area for eating in the kitchen with the perfect dining room. Bev was so excited she almost forgot to check out the bedrooms. All five of them.

When she walked upstairs, it was bright due to the skylight. She remembered saying, "this is too good to be true." The bedrooms were spacious, and they had huge walk-in closets. They were like apartments on each floor. All the bathrooms were good sized and beautifully decorated. Beverly walked into her master bedroom on the 2nd floor.

It took her breath away how the walk-in closet was like something out of a movie star's home.

When she went downstairs, and around the other side of the house, she could not believe that there were a large indoor swimming pool and a three-car garage. Beverly immediately knew this was her home.

Beverly asked the Realtor if she was sure that this listing was a townhouse and not a house? With all that space, she could not believe this fabulous place was in her price range too. She felt blessed.

Moving into a townhouse was a dream come true for Bev since she had lived in a comfortable apartment for years after her children were all grown.

Of course, decorating was going to be the most fun for her. She had been a big fan of the decorating shows on television for years. This is the townhouse that Beverly had lived in now for 19 years.

Beverly made it a habit of leaving earlier than necessary because she worked 40 minutes away and did not want to run into heavy traffic on the Highway which might cause her to be late.

In 15 years, she had only been late three times - lateness never looks good for an executive's image. After parking, in her reserved spot in the parking lot, Beverly grabbed her bags and entered the elevator to the 16th floor of the Main building.

The building was a glass building with the ability to see outside, but not able to see inside from the outside. The building was equipped with a gym that took up an entire floor, nurses' station, room to take a nap if needed and several cafeterias with ten cooks that took orders from the employees. It was a great place to work for sure.

Once off the elevator, she headed for her office saying her usual Good Mornings to her staff, also to those co-workers that were getting off the adjacent elevators.

The aroma from the Cafe at the end of the floor smelled so good that Beverly took a deep breath to take in the aroma of freshly ground coffee. Employees had a choice of hot or cold breakfast daily, and the food was always delicious if she had to say so herself.

Beverly waved to her co-workers as she made her way to the Cafe. Some of them joined her as they walked down the hallway.

Back in her office, Beverly thought to herself, *"this day is going to be a very long day,"* or maybe she was just a little anxious about her meeting.

Anyway, the work was somewhat slow today of all days. Carol, her assistant, came into the office with some notifications that needed her approval which she did quickly.

Just before lunch, the telephone rang, and Bev was

hoping that the C.E.O.'s Assistant Jennifer was calling her upstairs although she knew the meeting was set for 5 pm.

So, Beverly answered in her most professional voice, that's not to say she is not professional all the time, (but you'll know where she's coming from when you are expecting that certain call). We have different voices for different occasions like when you are expecting a call from your man you know you throw on that sexy voice, you know we can work the phone when it is necessary.

Well, the call was not from anyone at the job it was from her sister-friend Anita, and she sounded distressed, this had been her sister-friend for the last twelve years. Beverly knew she would have to sit down so she could understand and get all the details of whatever had upset Anita this much. Anita never calls Beverly at work unless it is an emergency.

Beverly thought to herself, *oh Lord, what has Anita so upset?* She asked Anita to calm down. Then Anita started telling Bev that Amber, Anita's only child, had been beaten up by her thug boyfriend, Jerome.

Jerome was a good-looking young man, resembling a young Melvin Gaye but had a thug attitude like "Little Napoleon." "What in the hell happened?!!" Beverly screamed so loud, she had to remember where she was. Beverly lowered her voice; it is a good thing her office door was closed.

Amber had this off and on relationship with this boy who neither Beverly nor Anita cared too much for him from the first time they met him.

Amber was in her junior year at college, a brilliant

student, but not when it came to picking boyfriends especially this one.

Beverly warned Amber about his attitude she had observed when he was around her, which made Beverly very uncomfortable. Anita always said, he was not good enough for her baby girl; however, as parents and aunties, we try to stay out of young folks' business.

Nevertheless, after hearing this, now it is their business, Jerome has gone too far, Lord help him. Once Anita told her ex-husband Reggie what happened to Amber his only daughter he was very, very upset. This guy had better leave the State or at least the neighborhood.

This situation is not going to turn out too good for this young man or young thug, whatever he wants to call himself.

While listening to the story, Beverly was torn between going to comfort her friend or stay for her important meeting. Beverly felt really bad for Amber, knowing all too well, *THERE IS NO REASON* for a man to put his hands on a woman especially violently.

Men are to protect their mate, care for and love them, not to abuse them physically or verbally. Love does not hurt. A man is to love a woman the way Christ loves the Church and the way he loves himself. Therefore, it is obvious that Jerome did not love himself.

Beverly sat in silence listening to her friend describe the entire event, according to what Amber had revealed to her mom, Jerome kicked her down, put his size 12-inch foot on her neck and punched her in her head and body and she blacked out for a few minutes.

When she became conscious, she was able to stand up although she was in pain, she was able to grab the broomstick that was leaning against the wall and when he was not looking, she slammed it against his head and the blow made a gash on his head, causing him to bleed.

Amber was sure her reaction shocked him, but that gave her enough time to run out of his apartment. She ran barefoot to her car that was parked across the street. Amber was shaking and crying, but by God's grace, she pulled together enough strength to drive herself to her mother's home.

She was banging on the door, which startled Anita and when she opened the door, she saw her daughter standing there shaking uncontrollably. Anita looked at her daughter and said, "My goodness what happened baby?"

Anita helped Amber into the house, sat her down on the couch and just held her but by this time, she was crying uncontrollably. Amber was trying to get the words together to tell her mother what had just happened.

Anita got up and got a warm cloth to put it on her forehead, and then brought her a warm cup of chamomile tea. The tea helped to calm Amber down enough so that she could start telling her mom the spine-chilling story of what happened between her and Jerome. Anita was just grateful that he had not killed her child.

"Sis," Anita said, "I wanted to run out and shoot the boy, but I know that was not the right thing to do." Once Amber found her composure, I drove her to the police station and told her to make a report on this guy. Amber was reluctant at first but once the police officer spoke with her, the woman officer convinced her it was for her safety that a report be filed and it was not anything that she had done that caused this reaction from Jerome.

Amber looked at her Mother and said, "mom, I'm so sorry." Anita's response was," I'm sorry too baby, but I'm glad that you're alive and safe."

Anita assured Amber that Aunt Bev and her dad would be here for her so she would not have to worry about this thug again.

Amber was terrified of what the outcome might be, but somewhere deep inside of herself, she knew her Mother was right.

Beverly was sitting at her desk with tears in her eyes because she was reflecting on her past abusive experiences and she never wanted Amber to experience any abuse especially not from a man or anybody else as far as that goes. "Well, Beverly said, "Sis, I'm glad she safe too."

Beverly expressed, "I feel bad about this; I just want to leave and come home and comfort you both, that is what I want to do right now, but you know I have this big meeting today. Are you going to be alright?" "Yes, Sis I will be fine?" Anita replied.

Anita told Beverly, "I am sorry to call you with this because I know this is a big day for you, but I had to tell you, I had to talk to someone." Although Anita had called and told her friend the troubling news, she assured Beverly that she had it under control and Amber was now laying down. Anita apologized again and told her she hoped to see her later. She wanted to know the exciting outcome from this meeting.

"Bev, I know you're upset, but go take a walk, calm down and grab some lunch because I know you haven't eaten. We've been talking for about an hour, and you need your energy." Anita ended by saying "To God be the Glory" that the fool did not kill our child." "Bye Sis, love you." "Love you too Sis, we will talk later for sure. I will stop by when I get off today." Anita said, "I know you will," and hung up.

Beverly had not realized that they had been on the phone close to an hour, Wow! She wanted to take a short walk to clear her mind and talk with the Holy Spirit for strength and clarity before the most important meeting of her life.

Beverly made it a priority to pray to the Holy Spirit before making any decisions. Beverly knew without a doubt that the Spirit of the Living God would go before her in this upcoming meeting and would show her favor.

Now lunch was completely over, and Beverly had forgotten all about eating. How could she eat after hearing this devastating news from her dearest friend?

After a short walk in the garden downstairs and time to reflect, Beverly's composure was back to normal or as normal as it was going to be today. After returning to her office, she remembered a line from a song sang by Pastor Cherry, "It Will Be Alright."

She sat down at her desk just thinking about how fortunate she was to have a great job and great friends. She started working on some reports that needed her signature, and she reviewed the stats from last week's reports.

The company was doing extremely well since she took over this division. Beverly was so involved in her work she did not pay attention to the time, so when the phone rang and her assistant Carol told her the call was from upstairs, she dropped everything to take the call.

The CEO's Assistant Jennifer asked her to come upstairs in about twenty minutes. They were running a little behind time because it was already 5:20 pm. Beverly thanked Jennifer thank and told her I'll be there in twenty minutes."

The CEO's office covered the entire 32nd floor, and not many staff members had met on this floor. When Beverly exited the elevator, she realized how classy this floor was every office had beautiful etched glass doors.

The carpet on the floor was a beautiful mint green and gray with gold-framed pictures of previous CEOs and top executives.

As she walked down the hallway, she wondered to herself if her picture would ever be hanging up among these top executives. When she walked up to the glass door, they opened automatically. Beverly thought to herself, *"Wow Impressive."*

Last time Beverly heard about the CEO he was a white man with silver hair who looked to be about 60 years old. or older. She had met him twice at two different company functions briefly, though much to her surprise this was not a man.

There had been a memo sent to the executives regarding the new C.E.O. that replaced Mr. Silverman, after his sudden death and this person was a tall 5'7, 150-pound, graceful Afro-American women. She was impeccably dressed in a gray pinstripe suit with shoes that must have cost close to $500.

The nameplate on the desk read, Erika Williams-Brownstone who was speaking on the phone indicated that Beverly take a seat across from her desk. As Beverly sat down, her mind began racing.

She knew that name from somewhere but where?

Beverly always remembered faces, but she could not quite place her face, but her name stood out. Now it was bugging her; she knew she would eventually remember.

"Oh Lord, help me," Beverly said in her mind. Beverly took a deep breath to stay calm. Once Ms. Brownstone ended the phone call their conversation was professional and open.

Erika knew Beverly's record of accomplishments and was very aware of her work ethics.

Mrs. Brownstone applauded Beverly for her dedication to her job. *"All right,"* she thought to herself, *she knows me. That is great, but why am I here in front of this woman? Is she in the position to promote anyone or is there someone else behind the scenes?*

One thing was for sure whoever she is she made it to a top position with this company and community, we take pride in her accomplishments.

Beverly tried to stay focused on the matter at hand and not gravitate to the past because now she remembered where she knew Ms. Erika Williams-Brownstone from.

They had crossed paths years ago, and it was not something that Beverly wanted to remember. Ms. Erika had not been very nice to Beverly in college. She constantly bickered with her in many of the classes they took together. Erika always thrived on attention and Beverly was comfortable in her skin.

Erika was a very light-skinned Afro-American young woman with long hair and hazel eyes, pretty face but not such a pretty personality at least not back in college. She showed she had a self-esteem problem back then, Well, she clearly filled her **VOIDS**.

To see Erika in this position Beverly was both happy and a little unsure. Then she thought, *"Alright Beverly, let bygones be bygones. We are two successful women."*

Ms. Brownstone started with small talk about the company, and how she transferred from another company, where she held a key position for ten years.

She understood why Beverly looked a little surprised when she saw her. However, Erika was fully aware of who Beverly was and her capabilities even before she recommended her for this position.

She had consulted with the Board of Directors as they reviewed her resume and evaluations over the years. They agreed with Erika that Beverly was the right person for the position. After the small talk, Erika said, "Alright let us get down to the business of why you have been chosen." Beverly thought to herself, *I think that's a good idea.*

"Ms. Beverly Jenson; I would like to offer you a position as CEO in our new division, which will have several smaller departments like youth training job preparations and drug abuse awareness classes. You can include whatever you feel that will be needed to make our division or should I say your new division successful. Should you accept this position, it will be a win, a win for the community and the company."

"I am aware that you have been running similar programs within this division for several years with quite an impressive outcome. The training programs that you developed and offered have inspired many of our youth. "Beyond Your View" program has benefitted so many young people in this city."

"I also know that you have a passion for youth and your executive skills have proven to allow your staff to work intensely to make those programs award-winning projects."

Your divisions have won several awards from the Mayor, and the Westchester and New York City Council. Many of the young people that enrolled in your programs have gone on to college and secured excellent jobs in top corporations."

"I have heard you speak in many of our Award-Winning dinners about how successful and how proud you are of the young people that your division worked with and how you want to continue to help our young people. Encouraging them to believe in themselves, our city and that they can become successful adults."

"Your speeches have touched the hearts of the Board Members and me. and other leaders throughout the state. So, this is the reason we wanted to offer you this position because I feel in my heart that you're the best person to run this new division besides, this staff loves you too, and that makes it a lot easier."

Erika took a deep sigh, and she went on to say that, she will explain the Pro's that come with this offer. "You get a hefty pay raise, $45,000 more which will bring you well over $175,000 per year in income."

"The company will provide you with a townhouse, a new car, and a personal travel expense account. The company will also pay three months' rent for you until you settle in. You still have all the benefits that you have here, none of them will change in any way trust me. So, how does this sound to you so far?"

Beverly was smiling by this time, and she said, "These terms sound inviting, but I'll need some time to take all this in before I can make my final decision." Beverly was thinking as she sat down and listened to what the company was offering.

She knew this was going to be a tough decision because, after twenty -something years of living in Westchester, New York leaving had never been an option. Beverly was about to ask a question when Ms. Brownstone said, "Oh I'm sorry I completely forgot to mention where we're hoping to open this new central office. It will be opening in Arizona, but the company is also looking into opening a division in Washington."

Beverly almost choked when she heard that, and she definitely knew that with this offer she had to re-evaluate and pray. She was not about to jump into any new venture without praying for guidance.

Many years before she accepted Jesus and His will for her life and she would not make decisions based on her feelings or how good the offer sounded.

Not realizing that the plan for our lives was made before we were even conceived. Remembering the Scripture from

Jeremiah 29:11. She knew that He (God) is the author of her life, and knew never again would she decide anything without waiting for God's guidance. Beverly had learned the hard way many times to wait on the Lord for answers.

"*Well?*" Erika looked at Beverly knowing she was thinking very hard about this offer and she went on to explain some more details about the project and what the Board of Directors was expecting from Beverly. Erika continued by telling Beverly that she would be allowed to make major decisions in the building and development of this project.

Erika asked Beverly, "Do you have any questions or comments, or do you want to wait for the next meeting? I think we can schedule it in about thirty days".

Thirty days would give Beverly a good amount of time to make up her mind, consult her pastor and write down any concerns that she might have.

Beverly's response to Erika was "You know Ms. Brownstone I have a lot to think over, and I appreciate that you have given me the thirty days to make my final decision. I will have a definite answer at our next meeting."

Ms. Brownstone stood up from behind her desk, and Beverly also stood up. They shook hands, and Beverly thanked her again for the meeting, and for offering her this opportunity. Erika walked from around her desk, and both ladies started walking through the glass doors to the elevators.

Beverly looked straight at Erika and said, "I love your suit, and those shoes are slamming!" They both laughed.

Erika then reiterated, "I know this is a big responsibility, but I'm also certain that you're the best person to take on this challenge, but please take the thirty days to review all aspects of this promotion.

We'll meet again next month. Have a great weekend Ms. Jensen." Beverly thanked her again and entered the elevator as Erika walked back to her office.

By the time, their conversation was over, Beverly knew Erika had changed in many ways. She was confident in who she is. In college, she strived to be the best or better than everyone else.

She has used that drive and determination to prove to herself that she would be victorious and her accomplishments with this company have shown that any woman with a goal and drive can make it in this world.

She was articulate and still an extremely attractive looking woman. As Beverly walked back to her office, she was thinking; *this could be a new beginning for her and her family.*

After Beverly's 16-year marriage with Xavier ended in divorce and the other obstacles that occurred this new venture could bring a new chapter in her life.

This position along with a new location could be a blessing to help more of the people she loved. The youth and opportunities that provided skills to the youth would make a new group of young achievers and believers in themselves. That is all she ever wanted to do is help people.

Beverly was excited thinking of all the good this

opportunity would provide for the company and the people of Washington or Arizona.

"Oh Lord," she thought, "We have traveled but never to Washington or Arizona." and she did not know much about either state. She was feeling so overwhelmed that she wanted to call everyone she knew and tell them the good news, but she knew that was not a good idea, not just yet.

Once back in her office she looked around, and most of the staff had left. That gave her some quiet time to catch up on some work. There was plenty of work waiting for her to review on her desk. She appreciated this because it would keep her from daydreaming or thinking too hard about the meeting she just left.

She knew that next week the entire office would be buzzing about the meeting but decided she wouldn't discuss this meeting with anyone.

Well, maybe her grown children but, definitely not anyone on the job. Beverly would work for about an hour and then head home.

An hour later Bev closed the door to her office and walked to where her car was parked.

While Beverly was driving, she started praying for guidance regarding this job offer. Beverly doesn't make any decisions anymore without praying until she gets an answer. She had faith that her answer would-be right-on time. God is always right on time in all of life's situations.

As Beverly drove up to her driveway, it seemed there were no lights on in the house. She thought to herself as she usually does, why in the world are all the lights out? It is not late. To make sure she was correct she checked the clock on the car dashboard. According to the clock, it was 7:39 p.m. somebody should be up. She stepped out of the car, unlocked the house door from the garage and walked into her house. "Hello! Where is everybody? Hello, my dear family."

Then she said to herself *"oh well"* maybe they are resting since they both had a rough day. All that mess with Amber and that guy Beverly did not even want to call him by his name.

Beverly walked into her spacious living room; she loved her beautifully decorated home. It was the colors of the sea and sand somewhere in the world, turquoise and gold. Plus, she had acquired expensive Black Art from some well-known artists. Her place was cozy, and that made her forget the worries of the day.

Amber was asking, "Who's that?" They both started laughing because who else would it be? Beverly asked. "Are you all out back?"

Amber responded, "Outside by the pool listening to some music and Mom grilled vegetables, shrimp, and salmon and your favorite salad, want some Auntie?" "Sure do," Beverly said, because I stopped and picked up some dessert."

Beverly heard the music and started dancing by the time she got to the bottom of the steps she was feeling good. She realized that it was a party just for the three of them.

This is the way to start three-day weekend. It felt good to not have to go to work until Tuesday. It's called kick back and relax. Not earlier, not later just in the moment.

Amber hugged her Aunt and just kept saying, "I'm sorry,

I'm sorry, I'm sorry Auntie." Beverly was a little confused at first, so this was the opening that we probably needed to discuss the situation that occurred earlier between Amber and Mr. Jerome.

They sat down and before the conversation Anita suggested, "First things first, let's eat." They all agreed, and Amber ran upstairs to get the plates, cups, and silverware.

Anita looked strangely at Beverly and said, "Girl, I know we're going to talk about your meeting with the CEO, right?" Beverly shook her head in agreement, but they both knew it would be later, much later for sure.

The only thing Beverly said was, "Girl, you won't believe who the CEO is! Wait until I tell you." Beverly was enjoying the music, and they all sat down to eat with little conversation because they wanted to appreciate every bite of this well-prepared meal. The moon was bright in the evening sky, and the warm breeze made for an enjoyable night.

Anita has always been a great cook, that is what inspired her to begin a catering business, and she's doing very well for herself too.

In her travels, she catered for very prestigious people; exclusive business owners, actors, and actresses, even catered for people in their neighborhood when they had events.

One of their favorite meals, succulent large grilled shrimp, salmon and asparagus with her homemade sauce and homemade lemonade that made all the others, a tease.

Amber started cleaning up while Beverly and Anita went to the other side of the patio and poured themselves some wine. Anita looked over at Beverly in a curious sort of way. Beverly smiled and said "Alright I'll tell you" they both started laughing.

"Sis, the meeting went very well. I was blown away by the details, but do you remember Calvin Hartman in college? You know the guy I messed around with for a few months, just to find out he was messing around with another girl at another college campus?"

Anita said "vaguely," After a few minutes, Anita said, "I do remember. I do because you didn't even bother getting upset like some of us would have. Some of the girls wanted to fight and scratch off the other girls' face and all of that, but you just dumped that guy. Why are you bringing him up?" Anita asked. Beverly said, "Remember Erika Williams? Well, now she's Erika Williams-Brownstone."

Anita still did not get the connection, "Okay Sis what does all this mean?" Anita asked. "Today, I had a meeting with the CEO whose name is Erika Williams- Brownstone."

Anita said, "You couldn't mean the same Erika we went to college with who stole your man! You cannot mean her."

"OH, my goodness, you mean her, What!!!" "Sis, you're always so dramatic!" Beverly was laughing. "Yes, Anita that Erika."

Anita look amazed, "I recall she was always trying extra hard to be noticed and accepted in school because she was nice looking. She was light skin with long hair, but she had low self-esteem. I guess that's what made her try to get with every guy on campus."

Beverly smiled then continued explaining to Anita, that after the conversation they had today, Ms. Erika Williams came a long way.

She's very secure in her position and what she wants. Erika worked extremely hard to get to the top. I applaud her, she's a CEO, and that's a great accomplishment for a black woman. Anita said, "That's a great accomplishment for any woman," Beverly said, "I'll drink to that."

Beverly went on to say, "She's climbed the corporate+ ladder to acquire the top position with our company and as I said before, the meeting did go very well I'm just not quite ready to discuss details yet."

"Well, Sis I understand and respect your decision on the matter because I know that you will be praying for guidance before you make any decisions about any aspects of your life," Beverly said, "You're so right about that Sis."

Anita said, "All right now onto the next subject, that will have to wait until tomorrow. I'm bushed, and it seems Amber hasn't come back down. I believe Amber feels the same way." Anita said, "Sis, I'm so thankful that she had sense enough to come straight here because she was a mess." Her voice began to tremble.

"I'm glad we have you in our lives you'll never know how thankful we are." Beverly looked Anita straight in her eyes and said, "Sis, I feel the same about both of you."

They stood up hugged one another, and Beverly said, "I'm headed for a warm bath and then the bed in that order."

Anita said, "Me too after I do some paperwork for a new client, I'll be working with next week." "Goodnight, Sis, get

some rest you deserve it. We'll talk tomorrow, Love you."
Bev replied, "Love you too."

Saturday started out damp and foggy. So, Beverly headed down to her gym which was in the basement. Beverly is big on staying healthy and fit, so her morning ritual keeps her body tight and her mind clear.

Exercise benefitted Beverly and it allowed her to think and look good at the same time. After a few minutes, Anita joined her and said, "It's always good to see you working out."

"After yesterday you probably need this more than I do." Beverly asked, "how's Amber doing this morning?" Anita said, "She still sleeping there were no classes today. You know we'll have to talk later regarding that close encounter of the abuse that she had."

Beverly reminded Anita that she felt so angry when she listened to the details of the event that went down because she never wanted Amber to experience abuse in any way. "You know that Nita." She said, we have tried to shelter her from that sort of thing. "You know we did," Anita said, "and it's not our fault."

Anita continued saying, "I'm not blaming myself or you, we have talked to her since she was a junior in high school, about these young boys and men. But there are some things, unfortunately, she'll just have to experience herself and hopefully, once she has, she'll learn from her mistakes like we all had to."

After a half an hour of exercising, they decided to

go upstairs, but they agreed they'd let Amber open the discussion on her terms and her own time. They didn't want to force the issue, and knowing Amber as they did, they also knew that she would pick the right time.

It's a long weekend, so this conversation will come up before the weekend is over. Surprisingly by the time they got to the top of the stairs the aroma from the kitchen caused them to smile at each other.

Amber was making Belgian waffles and bacon, which is everybody's favorite. Freshly squeezed orange juice was already on the table, and the coffee smelled great. Anita and Bev told Amber that they would take a quick shower and come down to enjoy Ms. Amber's breakfast.

Amber said, "Okay, I'll put the food on the warmer until you're ready." As they were about to go upstairs, Amber said, "Mom, Auntie, I want to talk about the other day." They both said alright Amber; we'll be down in a few.

After everyone had sat down and enjoyed the delicious breakfast and cleared the table Amber said, "Before I start, I just want to say I'm truly sorry for upsetting you both and I know without a doubt that both of you love me with every fiber in your being and I also feel the same way."

"I was beginning to feel uncomfortable around Jerome and wanted to break up with him, but when I told him how I felt he snapped! His reaction frightened me but down deep I knew he wasn't going to kill me.

Mom, I called on the name of Jesus and now I'm free. I wanted to contact my dad, but I was afraid of how he'd handle it."

"I have decided to make more time for studying and less

time for guys right now. I thank you both for understanding and respecting my feelings, I'm saying that to say that neither of you pushed me to discuss this, thank you for that."

She continued, well, I also called my college counselor who will assist me in signing up to become a mentor to a young person when I don't have classes if that's alright with you, Mom."

Anita smiled and said, "Amber I think that would be a wonderful thing to do - it's called paying it forward."

Beverly got up and hugged her niece and said, "I'm immensely proud of your decision. That all sounds positive to me, and you'll enjoy helping a younger person. You're following in Auntie's footsteps by helping young people, and it has been extremely rewarding in my career."

They picked up their glasses and toasted with orange juice and agreed that Amber had done the best thing getting the order of protection because this lets Jerome know that she's not playing with him.

Amber said that she received a call from Jerome saying he was sorry exactly what Beverly told her he would do.

Amber told him, "I'm finished with you. I'll be changing my beeper number so don't try and contact me," The last thing Jerome told Amber was he's moving back to Washington next week. But I'm not responding to any of his calls. Beverly said, "Good for you, baby girl."

The next morning turned out to be sunny and cool and the birds were singing, a sound that Beverly loved to hear. She always thought that the birds were singing to God.

She was going over in her mind the conversation she had with Amber early that morning. Beverly thought to *herself that her Amber was growing into an intelligent young woman.*

She was proud of her decision to volunteer her time to tutor a young person, who may not be able to afford a tutor. Volunteering is a blessing.

This was a good time to go shopping before the weather changed into a bad rainstorm. Beverly wanted Amber to go with her since Anita had a meeting with a client for a wedding reception. She knew that Amber enjoyed shopping and Anita agreed that would make her day.

So, Beverly went upstairs and asked Amber if she wanted to go with her, knowing that Amber would never turn down a day out with her Aunt Bev.

Amber was excited to spend some quality time with her Aunt at the Mall because her Auntie would buy her almost anything, she wanted which is something Bev had been doing for several years now.

Amber overheard the conversation and before Bev could finish her sentence, Amber told her "I'll be ready in 20 minutes alright?"

Beverly laughed to herself. *"Alright, I'll be downstairs.* Come down when you're ready."

Beverly heard Amber say, "Okay, I'm checking the weather first. Beverly yelled upstairs, "I already did, Amber. I want to go and get back before the rainstorm."

Twenty minutes later Amber was dressed and ready to go. Bev grabbed her bag, and they both went to the car and headed to the Mall which was about a good half an hour away on a good day.

While they were driving, Amber said, "Can I say something?" Of course, you can tell me anything baby girl." "Auntie, Mom wasn't as upset as I thought she would have been. I was scared to tell her at first, but she surprised me, and so did you. Neither of you were upset or condemned me. Why was that Auntie?"

Beverly was glad Amber asked this question because it gave her a chance to express her feelings on the matter. "First of all, Amber, we were grateful that the fool didn't kill you or critically injure you. Secondly, you did the right thing in a very wrong situation, got away, got home, and told your mother what happened."

"You were willing to report the incident to the authorities, so there was no reason for us to be upset with you. It was the situation that was upsetting but, it was not your fault. You made all the correct decisions proving to us that you can handle any situation that you may have to face on your own."

"We love you, and we continually pray for God to protect you. So, although Jerome did hurt you, you're still with us, and that alone is a blessing, and I have to say that I'm very proud of the decisions that you've made."

Amber's eyes were watery, and a tear ran down her cheek.

Beverly touched her face and said, "we love you baby girl

and don't ever forget it." Amber had tears running down her face, but she managed to say, "I love you too Auntie."

The Mall was not as crowded as Beverly had anticipated it would be, or maybe young people were just getting up, considering it was 10 A.M. and a Saturday. She knew by noon the scene would change.

Amber walked into one of the shoe stores and was checking out some boots. She loved boots. Beverly said, "Amber I'm going to the Home store just to browse, catch up with me when you're finished browsing." "Okay, Auntie." She heard Amber voice although she didn't see her.

Beverly ran into a few of her co-workers, they stopped, had small talk and then Beverly continued to the store. She wasn't looking for anything in particular, but if something caught her eye, she'd check it out. Beverly had become a smarter shopper. She had disciplined herself when she shopped by saying to herself *"Is this something I want or something I need*

Before she learned that trick, she would overspend and would be taking things home that she either already had or didn't need. There were many times she found herself taking things back to the store and it kept the credit card bills lower. At one time Beverly shopped to fill a **VOID** and that's a costly habit.

When Amber caught up with Beverly, she had a strange look on her face. Beverly said, "Amber are you alright? "Amber looked up at her with tears in her eyes. "Honey, what's wrong? What happened in the store? Did someone bother you? What is it?" Amber wiped her eyes and said, "Auntie, I just saw Jerome with a girl and a baby. How could he?"

Beverly sternly looked in her face and said, "Amber stop crying right now!!!"

"Don't let him get you upset, at least now you see for yourself who he is. He's no good for you". Amber gave her a side smile because that statement made her bounce right back. Beverly knew she'd be alright when she said, "Auntie did you find anything nice for the house?"

Beverly told Amber you know I didn't look, so let's look together, so they walked down the aisle of the store. Time went by so fast, and before they knew it, it was close to three o'clock, and they realized they were famished.

"Hey, let's get back to the house before the weather gets worse". Beverly suggested. It had already begun to rain harder while they were still in the Mall and by the look of the clouds as they were about to leave the storm was on its way. "Auntie I just wanted to stop and pick up a blouse I saw."

"I wanted your opinion on it before I bought it", "OH!" Beverly said, "My opinion counts now missy?" They laughed and walked back to the store. When Beverly saw the blouse, she said, "Wow, it's nice. I like It".

Amber said, "Oh good because I do too and I found a skirt that goes perfectly with it, and I've already tried them on, and they look cool together. I'll be back in a minute I'm going to tell the sales lady I'll be taking them both."

Beverly had already begun walking toward the customer's cashiers' line, waiting for her niece. She smiled and asked the cashier, "Is there a sale today?"

Meanwhile, Anita got a call from Amber's father, who was Anita's ex-husband Reggie. He was so upset, asking her "Why would you let our daughter date this older guy," Anita cautioned, "calm down Reggie and don't put this on me. For one thing, our daughter is grown and capable of making her own decisions on some aspects of her life".

Without responding to her, he went on to say: "Well, I confronted him about him hitting my daughter, and he tried to say it was a mistake. We exchanged a few choice words, and my choice was to leave him broken and busted up. His choice! I had to use some handiwork on that thug, but he got the message."

Anita said," I hope you didn't hurt him badly? Tell me you didn't Reg". Reggie didn't respond to her question either. Anita, Reggie continued, "she's never to see him again, and I mean it." "Reggie calm down. I can promise that won't be happening and before you ask; yes, we reported it to the police."

"Good, Reggie said "I've got to go, but I'll call her later. Nita, she'll always be my little girl no matter how old she gets." Anita said, "I know Reggie. I know and I feel the same way". They both hung up simultaneously.

Beverly told the cashier to ring up everything. "Oh wait, Auntie looks there a nice watch and a ring that would look great with this outfit." By the time they left the store, Amber had walked out with five new outfits. It was pouring rain by this time.

Driving home was a little difficult, but they made it safely. When they got to the house, Anita was cooking up a storm in the kitchen, and because they were hungry, they didn't waste any time washing up, preparing to eat.

Anita asked, "Amber well girl how was your day with Auntie Bev was it great as usual? Amber said, "wait until I show you all my new outfits. Oh Mom, guess who I saw at the Mall?" Anita thought for a moment then answered, "Who, some of your school friends, or some cute guys?"

Amber shook her head, "No Mom, I saw Jerome with a girl and a baby, that "THAT TWO-TIMING BUM.""

Anita's response was, well, Amber that just goes to show you he was never good for you anyway and what we do in the dark always come to light. By the way, your dad called while you girls were out shopping. "Oh, my goodness Mom! Was he upset?"

"Yes, Amber he was terribly upset, and I had to calm him down just to listen to his side of the story. By the end of the conversation he was calmer, though, he said, he'll call you later and He'll be out of town on the road for a while."

Anita thought to herself, *Over the years Amber had gotten close to her biological father and even closer after David her stepfather was killed.*

After eating they all cleaned up the kitchen and Beverly decided to go upstairs to do some much-needed reading.

That allowed Amber to spend some time with her mom and she was excited to show off all her new outfits.

At about 10 o'clock that evening Amber got a call from one of her girlfriends that attended college with her. It was Valerie. She said, "Hey Amber it's me, Val, how are you doing? Guess what I just found out about Jerome? "Amber said, "Girl, I'm not even interested in finding out. Amber wait, I've got to tell you this." Amber said, Okay, Okay with a sigh, what's up? Val went on to tell Amber, girl, I heard he got beat up by some guys. They beat him up because he was hitting on some girl in the street and I heard they beat the heck out of him too.

Amber said, "well I guess he deserved it." She was not about to reveal to her friend what Jerome did to her. Wow! Amber said with no emotion in her voice, it's called Karma. What goes around comes around, and sometimes it doesn't take too long."

Even though Amber couldn't see Valerie, she could just imagine the look on her face. Valerie was frowning and couldn't quite understand why Amber made that statement, or maybe she knew something about Jerome that Valerie didn't.

They continued their conversation with casual talk about school. The girls talked about everyone they could think of for the next hour and a half before hanging up.

Even though Beverly had Friday off the weekend still seemed to move quickly. Everybody woke up early to get ready for church on Sunday. They all enjoyed church.

Pastor D.E. Wright was the pastor of the church they attended, and she always gave a great powerful, and meaningful sermon to start your week off right. She was truly an anointed woman of God. You felt it in her hands, you saw it in her smile and knew it through her worship.

Beverly always believed that God had sent her to Pastor D.E. Wright because not only did they share the same middle name Elizabeth, but due to the love she poured on everyone Beverly would grow spiritually, and emotionally. And she did only through the wisdom God had given this amazing woman, friend, and Pastor.

Anyone that knows her teaching had to grow spiritually because she encouraged you and saw in a person what that person might not had believed they could achieve. She is a gifted woman and Beverly had been under her wings was remarkably close to her for several years now, which helped her build a strong foundation in the Lord.

They have worked together on many of the projects that the church sponsored. Although Beverly has spoken to her pastor about the new developments regarding her job offer, she was pondering about a one-on-one with her pastor soon to express her feelings about leaving the church that Beverly loved.

That might have been the one thing Beverly wrestled with about making this move. Beverly, Anita, and Amber have grown to love their church and the church family.

So, relocating would not be easy for any of them, especially Amber. She's in the choir and a youth counselor, and both Anita and Beverly believe that this is what keeps her grounded.

The youth that attended this church were so involved with the Youth Programs. Beverly wondered how Amber found time for a boyfriend in the first place. Anyway, we all know where there's a will there's a way when it comes to young people.

Even though her Pastor would always be her pastor, being that far away would make it difficult to find another church and church family like the one she has now. Sadness came over her just thinking about this, Beverly thought, *was this God's plan for her?*

Filling a **VOID.**

After service, they would go to eat at the Chinese buffet or a restaurant of Pastor's choice. It was always a great time to fellowship and enjoy each other outside the church. The Pastor would always have something funny to talk about that made everyone laugh so hard their sides would hurt by the end of the meal.

Beverly thought, *where would she find that kind of church family?* She didn't believe she could, so leaving would be a hard decision for her to make.

Yes, it was a great opportunity, yes it was more money, yes, it's all those extra bonuses, but the reality was, did she in her heart want to leave New York?

As they were leaving the restaurant, the Pastor grabbed Beverly by the hand and said to her, "How are things going with that promotion?"

Beverly responded, truthfully, the promotion is exciting

but before she finished the sentence, her Pastor looked at her and said, Bev, make an appointment with me as soon as possible because we need to talk about this and the sooner, the better. Bev said, "That's so true, alright, Pastor will do, love you and have a good evening."

Pastor laughed saying, "I will as soon as I get home and take a nap," laughing on the way to her car, where her husband waited for her, then they pulled off. Beverly walked over to her car and blew kisses in the air at everyone and off she went.

While sitting in her car Beverly thought to herself, *that she needs to think this opportunity through because what she's realizing is, that it's not just her, she has Amber and Anita to think about also.*

Her concern wasn't with her grown children because they have their lives so they would agree with her decisions no matter what, but about Anita and Amber because they were family too. There is more to this move than meets the eye. Beverly didn't know what that saying meant, but she heard it all her life.

Anita and Amber were going to visit her ex-husband's parents whom she was still close to. They were Amber's grandparents and they loved their granddaughter.

Mr. and Mrs. Burgess have been married for 50 years and still happy and frisky if you know what she meant.

Anita made sure she called them before going over because sometimes they would just get up and travel and never tell anyone where they were or when they would return. So, Anita learned to call first just to make sure they were home.

As they pulled up in front of the house, Frances was standing in the doorway with open arms waiting to hug her girls, as she likes to call them.

"Grandma Fran," Amber yelled, "You Look Fly." Her grandmother laughed. Fran said, "Child stop it; you know I always look good. Look at my girls, Frances said and invited them inside for a cool drink. Make yourself at home. You know where everything is, so don't expect me to serve you, as she busted out in laughter.

Fred and Frances were as opposite as any couple could be. Frances was always talking and laughing while Fred was more reserved and laid back. It must have made for a perfect marriage after 50 years.

Fred was 6' tall with red hair and freckles, loves to cook and loves his wife. He was always joking saying he's a Black Irishmen. Frances was 5'3," but she was always stricter than Fred when their kids were growing up.

Frances was a petite lady, curvy but not fat and she loved to dance. Frances was a dancer for years before she started a family, then she devoted all her time and energy to them. Everyone said they made a cute couple, even now.

Anita said when she first met them Frances never seemed to age but she'll tell you she's old enough to know better.

Women don't have to tell their age, but Fred would say, "Honey you know you're 72 years old, hell I'm 76 myself, so yes baby, we're old."

He'd smile and sit down in his favorite chair, reaching for the remote looking for a basketball or football game.

Fred was an architect and designed some incredibly famous landmark buildings in his day. Many remain standing today in different states around the country.

Frances had recently retired from a nursing career. She taught nursing for many of the student nurses around major hospitals in New York State and the surrounding areas.

Isabel their oldest daughter and a nurse who followed in her mother's footsteps lives in Maryland; she is the mother of the twin girls. Amber and Isabel's twin girls could pass for triplets they looked so much alike.

Amber was their third granddaughter, following the twin girls the first granddaughters. Their sons Earl and Jason recently got married, well not recent but about three years ago, and they both have sons.

Earl and his wife live in Georgia, so taking vacations are what Fred and Frances look forward to doing as much as possible. Earl has two sons, and Jason just had a newborn son. Jason lives in California not far from the beach, so Fred and Frances go there every summer for a least three weeks.

Retirement allows them to visit children every chance they get. The twins are both career-minded young women, a few years older than Amber, but they constantly keep in touch with their grandparents.

Reggie the oldest son joined the service right out of school but once he was deployed to Vietnam, that's when the trouble started. Anita barely recognized her husband after the war.

He came back a different person (and was still married

to Anita). He drank and gambled too much and verbally abused her too much. His mother always said, "The war destroyed my son."

Later he started using crack cocaine and that along with everything else Anita had experienced with him finally destroyed their marriage. Anita couldn't take any more.

Crack turned Reggie into a paranoid monster, always seeing things that only he saw or heard. Reggie was always accusing his wife of cheating with the next-door neighbor or the postman or just a random stranger. Truthfully, that was something Anita would never have done. She loved her husband even in his mess; she prayed for God's intervention.

The enemy was destroying a marriage that was once a beautiful union; it was also destroying her as well. Finally, she had to make some hard decisions about how this situation was making her feel. Mostly how was it affecting their daughter. Amber watched her daddy act strange to the point of cussing and sometimes arguing for no reason which often caused Amber to have nightmares.

It was a painfully confusing time for both. Anita prayed for guidance and one night the Spirit of the Living God spoke to her and told her to leave. Her husband didn't want to change or get help.

Many days she would drive over to talk with Fred and Frances about their son, but they knew and agreed with her that it was time to let it go.

Frances would say, "Baby, if Reggie wants you as his wife, he got to get his life right with Jesus first, then with his family and right now we don't see that happening."

That white witch (crack) as she is referred to it had taken

a good man and made him a mean, uncontrollable man. He had gotten locked up several times for auto theft and robbery something he would have never done in his right mind.

Fred interjected his feelings by saying, "You have to love yourself and your child more than you love your husband now, honey." Anita remembers sitting in their living room crying her eyes out sobbing so hard she could hardly breathe, but she knew they were right.

Her Reggie, the man that she thought she would be together with until death do us part, had parted them, changes that made her not only scared for herself and her child, but she was also scared for him.

Only the Lord knows, what he was doing to get that next fix. He lost his job, car and never had money, prior to this he made good money because he drove tractor trailer trucks for a living.

Anita and Amber never wanted for anything however, things had changed drastically, and Anita knew what she had to do. Deep down this was hurting her more than anything she had ever experienced.

Anita had given this man 21 years of her life they were high school sweethearts. She was devastated by what had happened in the last eight years. It hurt her deeply. Fred said, "Honey, Reggie chasing the devil and he's winning. For now, he's winning for now. It will change, I believe God will save him."

Frances would tell them stories about the patients that came into the hospitals where she worked and how that horrible drug made so many people of all colors and creed try and suicidal, and how families were separated because of this horrendous drug.

Children were being put in foster care straight from the hospital after the mothers were giving birth to these crack addicted babies. Frances said she used to cry because it hurt to see this on a continual basis.

Well, Anita would always stay connected to these two beautiful people not only because they were her daughter's kin but also because they loved her, and she loved them too. Anita had lost so much in her life.

Her sister Theresa to Lupus, her brother Michael to a motorcycle accident and her second husband David to the war. She was always trying to Fill a **VOID.**

We all have **VOID's** in our lives and how we choose to fill them can make us a better person or destroy us all together. Anita filled hers by cooking and making her world better for herself and her child, but not without the help of Jesus Christ. Not without learning to put her trust and faith in Him. Not without giving her pain, hurt and disappointments to God.

Because when she thought she could do it alone, she realized she couldn't; She wasn't strong enough, smart enough or wise enough.

But we can do all things through Christ… (Philippians 4:13)

She knew Jesus could handle all her burdens and free her to make a new start.

Having a family like Fred, Frances, and Beverly by her side Anita had become victorious and found peace and joy by finding Christ. Amber and Anita stayed for dinner with her in-laws, Mrs. Frances would not have had it any other way. Amber was in the kitchen when Frances said, "Baby girl, your father was furious about that young man, although he didn't call him that."

Amber was shocked, "Oh NO!" She said, "Daddy told you, grandma?" I'm sorry grandma I've made a mess of things. "Hey young lady just wait a minute; you're not blaming yourself for his actions, I hope? He's a man and knew what he did to you wasn't correct. So, don't you dare blame yourself!

You better not. You hear me, baby girl." Amber humbly answered, yes grandma. "It's his loss, look at you, young and sexy like your grandma (she laughed), smart too, and that knucklehead didn't know who you were. Frances continued expressing her thoughts to Amber and grandpa was shaking in head in agreement. He's crazy even to think that abusing you was wise I was scared for that young man because I know how my son can get when it comes to his baby girl. You might as well know he may now know that I made your father promise me he wouldn't kill that boy.

"Honey you're a queen and any man that you deal with better know that. Okay!! Don't lower your standards and don't settle. If they want you, they better bring it, and they better have something to bring not just no ding-a-ling either!" Amber was blushing at this point. But if she knew anything about her grandma, she knew she didn't bite her tongue.

Fred was the chef in the family, so he made everyone's favorite: turkey meatloaf, mashed sweet potatoes, and fresh spinach.

At the table, Amber told her grandparents about her decision to volunteer her time to tutor young people and leave boyfriends in the background for a while.

Fred said, "That's my girl! See she's growing up to be quite a young lady" and Frances agreed. Anita replied, "I'm proud of my baby girl, no, let me correct that our baby girl" and they all said Amen to that.

After dinner, Amber helped grandma clean up the kitchen and they had small talk. They talked about Beverly and how busy she been lately with her work, she works hard, and she travels almost every month.

Amber told her grandma how proud she is of her mother's accomplishments too. She works long hours, and sometimes I help her. and Frances was delighted to hear this good news and told Amber to make sure she sends her love to her Auntie Bev too.

Within the hour Reggie knocked on the door, and Amber was surprised to see him and a little worried that he was going to fuss at her.

But to her surprise, he hugged her and said, "That thug ex-friend of yours is not to come near you ever again."

Amber answered him with, "Dad, I know, he won't I promise." And it was left at that. He kissed his parents and made small talk with Anita and told them he's on the road again for probably the next two or three months.

He was also celebrating his sobriety for the eighth year, "Mom and Dad, I'm clean and sober, and it feels great!"

Everyone said, "Congratulations keep up the good work.

Reggie told his Father, I'm very grateful for you because you and mom understand my struggle, and I know I'm better for it. Reggie glanced over at his beautiful daughter who shook her head in agreement.

Reggie finally got his life back on track, and now he's back to doing what he loved driving those big rigs.

Anita likes it too because he is paying all his back-child support for his daughter every month and a nice amount too, $450 weekly, not bad if she had to say so herself. He had promised that once he got himself together, he would contribute and help her any way he could and had gone as far as to ask if they could get back together.

Anita wasn't comfortable with that idea yet. She wasn't so sure they could make it work again after so much had gone on between them.

So, they agreed to keep things the way they were for now. Anita asked him, just be a good father to your daughter that should be our main concern and Reggie agreed.

Amber and Anita hugged Fred and Frances and told them they would see them soon. "Grandma takes good care of my favorite grandpa." I love you both see you." They walked out and got in the car and headed home.

In the car, Amber said, "Mom, thanks, I needed to talk with my grandma she always tells me just what I need to hear." Anita glanced at her daughter admiring her and said, "She always did baby girl. That's called love and wisdom."

"I hope Auntie Bev had a good day too. Did she say what she'd be doing today?" "No, but I'm sure she had a good day," Anita said, "Do you need to stop by our house or straight to auntie's? Mom I don't think I have that much more to get from our place, most of my stuff is upstairs at aunties place." Anita replied, Alright, then we're headed to auntie's place.

"Mom, are we staying with Auntie for good?" "Yes, Amber we are, would you like that?" Anita asked, "Yes," "Mom that's a great idea."

"I honestly don't want her to be in that big house alone, besides, I love the pool and backyard. Don't you mom?" "Yes, I must agree with that honey. She's been asking me when we were moving completely in, now I'll tell her we will very soon."

How does that sound? "It sounds G-R-E-A-T, mom."

They both laughed and sung along with the songs playing on the radio. "Mom." Amber said, "It was great to see my grandparents, and do they ever get old mom? How could they look the same way they looked two years ago?" We heard them say that he's 76 years old. He doesn't look 76, does he?" "No honey he sure doesn't."

Amber asked, "it's still early we have any plans?" "I'm not sure, wait until we get home and see what your auntie wants to do. Okay, mom, that sounds good." Well, this weekend was almost over, so it was back-to-school for Amber and back to work for Anita and Beverly. Anita has clients to meet tomorrow while checking out sites for her restaurant and catering business.

While Anita was heading back to Beverly's place which would soon be their place she thought about Reggie. *He did look good like his old self, sexy she thought and smiled.*

Meanwhile Beverly was in the backyard taking a cool dip in the pool, in fact, she loved her home.

As Beverly stepped out of the pool, she dried off and sat in her lounge chair thinking about the week ahead. She had contemplated that when she returned to the office, the other employees would be gossiping and there would be buzzing around the water fountain about the meeting, and the outcome.

The weeks passed by quickly and the next meeting was coming up, but Beverly still hadn't made a final decision, but she knew she needed to make one ASAP. She still needed to speak with her advisor, her Pastor.

By the time they got back to the house, everyone was happy to see each other.

"Auntie, we went to visit my grandparents and they sent their love. They were happy to see us, and I saw my dad while we were there too. He made me promise not to ever see Jerome again; you know I did."

"You know how he would have gotten if I didn't. He told me when he gets back, we'll spend the weekend together and go up to the cabin. I hope he gets back soon even though he did say three months, right mom?"

Well, now that everyone was home, they would get prepared for the next work and school week. Beverly usually gets her wardrobe ready for the week. This way she has time to exercise and spend time meditating on the Word before she heads out to the job. Beverly's closet is organized by colors, all blues, greens, and gold tops together, and so forth and so on.

She always attempted to stay organized professionally

and in her personal life as well. This allowed Beverly to think with clarity and to be more creative. It had worked for many years so why would she change it now?

Well, it's Tuesday, and the office is up and busy as usual. Carol, Beverly's assistant, informed her that she would have to travel to Dallas, Texas this week for an Annual Executive Leadership Conference.

An emergency meeting was called due to the Junior Executive having to go to the General Safety Training Session and all this occurred at the same time, emergency after emergency. She asked, Carol to make the arrangements for her and let her know what time her flight was.

Carol informed her that the paperwork for her trip was being arranged as they spoke. "Ms. Jensen, sorry for the short notice. I just received this information late last night on my answering machine."

Beverly told Carol we're used to these short notifications by now. It's not your fault. Oh, and I almost forgot to tell you, Mr. Sheppard will be accompanying you.

Before Beverly could say anything, Carol next question was, "Would you like to stay at the same hotel you stayed at the last time you were there?" Beverly sighed and said, "that's a great idea, that hotel has a lot to offer I enjoyed staying there."

"Carol is there anything else we need to discuss?" Beverly smiled and looked up at her assistant smiling, Carols' response was No, we have covered everything.

Alright, I know you'll take care of everything, thank you, Carol, as a matter of fact, please set-up a conference call with Mr. White, he is the C.E.O and board member to discuss whatever problems I'm walking into. Thanks."

She knew she always had mixed feelings when it came to this trip. It seemed like there was always more issues than what had been discussed on the conference calls.

Hopefully, this trip won't run into the timeframe set up for her next meeting, because the last trip ended up lasting three weeks before the issues were resolved. She felt blessed that her staff worked independently, well at least when she had to go out of town.

After not one but three conference calls and a quick meeting with the supervisors, Beverly informed them that she would be traveling and what she expected from her staff while she was gone.

All her supervisors were confident and experienced with the procedures, so she was never worried about her division. They had proven themselves that *"while the Executives' away some mice won't play."* It was midday, and there was still an overload of work to be reviewed.

Beverly, Carol and three of the seven supervisors would be reviewing the workload before final plans were made for this trip. While they were involved in review Johnathan Sheppard, the C.E.O. of the Corporate Planning Division walked in, "Hello, Ladies. Wow, you all look terribly busy. Can I borrow Ms. Jensen for a few minutes?"

Beverly stepped away from the table of the adjoining office and walked into her office with Mr. Sheppard. "Have a seat, Johnathan. What's on your mind?" We have an important trip, the Executive Conference. Well, not even a whole week if you don't count the weekend." Johnathan begun explaining there was another serious issue in the lower Manhattan office.

They're having a lot of employee calling out sick, and the company is concerned that they might have to shut the agency down due to poor performance. Their production is continuously dropping monthly.

Most of the employees have been employed with the division for at least 12 to 15 years.' However, we need to modernize the facility for better service and productivity. I wouldn't like making people choose between looking for work elsewhere or relocating if it's not necessary for them to do so. Do you agree Bev?"

Beverly's responded, "Johnathan, the last time I visited the Manhattan office it wasn't in good condition then. So surely by now, it's close to being unsafe and unhealthy."

"I thought we had discussed those conditions with the Board before. Didn't they take any of our suggestions into consideration then?" Johnathan said, "Well did they?" They both shook heads, "NO!" I'll get two of my top managers down there immediately."

"Well alright, then we'll meet next week for the conference, not sure of the day yet but it's quite warm in Dallas, so let's make ourselves comfortable and professional at the same time." Beverly cleared her throat to say, "I know you're not telling me how to dress, Mr. Sheppard are you?"

Johnathan smiled and replied, "Of course not you're a Fashionista Ms. Jensen, then they both laughed. "Let me get back to the work at hand; my staff is waiting for me."

"Later Bev," Johnathan said, and he left as quickly as he had arrived. Beverly made some notes of their conversation and handed it to Carol. Beverly's mind was racing. *The promotion, the sudden emergencies, and Mr. Sheppard and all in a short time span.*

Beverly returned to her office and resumed where she left off reviewing reports, but Carol had something that she had to express to Beverly that might not make her so happy. "Ms. Jensen, I found miscalculations in two of the reports that had never shown up before."

Beverly frowned and said, "explain what you've found." Yes, of course I will Carol said as she rose from her chair to sit closer to Beverly. They both went over the reports from the Manhattan office, and sure enough, where Carol had put notations there were errors.

These reports will be forwarded to the analysis department for further investigation. Carol, please prepare these reports to be delivered to the correct department. This is now out of our jurisdiction.

Carol responded by telling her boss, "I prepared the forms while you were meeting with Mr. Sheppard". Beverly shook her head Carol, took her job seriously, as did most of her staff.

Beverly hoped that this was just an error on the report and nothing else like fraud. She has had to fire two supervisors after a thorough investigation recently found that they were forging numbers for uncompleted staff reports. That was the dirty part of the job or any job for that matter.

Undoubtedly this is a serious offense, and she and the company did not stand for any misleading information especially if she oversaw these divisions. Audits will be ordered immediately.

Beverly wanted everything to be in order before she left for this emergency trip. "Ladies let's break for a late lunch and meet back in an hour and a half to finish up these stats." Everyone agreed and left the office. These reviews always took the entire day to complete and sometimes it took two days.

Meanwhile, Carol went back to her office and checked the incoming messages just to find out that the Dallas trip was in two days.

The Board of Directors' secretary had left the message and informed Carol to open her email and review the details of the trip for both Mr. Sheppard and Ms. Jensen.

After reading the email, Carol immediately contacted Beverly to make her aware of this development. She also forwarded the email to Mr. Sheppard's assistant.

After these details had been given to Beverly and Johnathan, they were on the phone discussing their opinions, but it didn't matter how they felt, the Board had chosen them to represent the company, and that was final. Johnathan told Beverly; you know it hasn't been long since I've returned from Japan.

The Board is in the process of investigating business ventures with them also since they have developed technology that we have caught up with here in the U.S. I'm the only executive that speaks Japanese, Konnichiwa means Hello in Japanese. *He laughed to himself. "You didn't know that did you, Bev?"*

"No, John I didn't, but I'm glad you let me in on that

important detail. However, we'll be leaving for Dallas in two days. I've got to pack and make last minute preparations for my staff. Do you want me to pick you up at your place or will you pick me up, John?"

Beverly knew how he was; she already knew he would be picking her up three hours early before the flight since the airport was quite a distance from where he lived but closer to her side of town.

Johnathan said," I'll pick you up at 5:30 a.m. Thursday morning. Is that good for you my lady? At least we're flying first class as always," I love this company don't you." "We'll talk later because I have to finish these reports before leaving." "Yes, Beverly I do too, Bye."

After hanging up Beverly took a minute to reflect on how fast life can change, but she was never surprised. *Our God never changes she thought, thank God you never change Lord.*

At the end of the day, Beverly Jensen felt that the audits were finished. The one report with the incorrect stats had been sent to the correct department to be re-evaluated and now it's time to head home and pack for this trip.

When Bev reached her home, she felt exhausted, and she did not feel like having any long conversations. Amber was home, but when she saw her Auntie, she immediately knew this was not a time to have any discussions with her.

Amber said, "Auntie just relax I'll bring you something to eat if you want, do you, I mean, want something to eat?" "Yes, I would love that, thank you. It's been a hectic day."

Amber said, "I can tell." A few moments later Amber

handed her a tray to set her plate on. "Amber, I'm leaving for Dallas, in a few days for an Annual Executive Conference."

"I would like you to help me pick out some dresses because as you know, it always uncomfortably hot in Dallas." Amber was excited to help but was also feeling sad that Bev had to go. She always missed her when she left even for a short time. Amber reassured Beverly by saying, we'll be fine while you're gone, but you already know how much we'll miss you."

Beverly gave her niece a hug and said I'll miss both of you too. Hopefully, we won't have to stay too long. Amber said, "WE?" They laughed, and she said, "Yes Missy, WE! Mr. Sheppard will also be going." As they were talking Anita came in saying "Hi everyone."

I had an eventful day with my new clients. How about your day?" They both said theirs was complicated. Amber couldn't wait to tell Anita that Beverly was on her way to Dallas with Mr. Sheppard.

"Oh, that should be interesting," Anita said smiling. Bev said in a warning voice, "Sis don't go there it's all work related." "All work and no play make Bev a dull girl," now Anita explained laughing.

Anita walked in the kitchen to put away the groceries she had brought in. Beverly said, "Come on Amber we got work to do!"

There was a gold journal on Beverly's nightstand, "Auntie, do you write in that journal every day?" I'm asking because I write in mine every day too." "Yes, Amber, I've been keeping journals for many years since I was young. My deepest secrets are in those books."

"Could I read them one day Please?" Beverly hesitated because she couldn't really answer that question. She thought to herself, *why did Amber want to read her journals? They are closed chapters in her life that she wasn't sure she wanted to share or explore ever again.*

"Amber, I'll have to think about it, but for now, I'm not sure that's such a good idea."

Amber rebutted, "I think I'd love to get to know you when you were young, I mean younger cause you're still young. I bet there are some S-T-O-R-I-E-S about the fun things you did when in your youth."

Beverly didn't want to continue with this conversation. Amber not a good idea like I said. Amber looked oddly at Beverly because the tone of her voice let her know she didn't want to talk about those journals anymore.

"Alright, Auntie maybe another time, I know you're tired, I'll leave so you can get your rest." She was walking toward the door, Good night Auntie "Good night baby girl."

Later, Beverly was laying in her bed thinking to herself; *Lord, those journals have so much of my past, too much of her pain, sorrow, and shame.*

She wasn't sure if Amber would even understand why she works so diligently to achieve, to maintain a standard of life that many years ago they said she would never have, she would never be anything. She would etc...

She remembered thinking all the lies they told her. She was somebody, she may not have known WHO, but she knew she was different.

Now she knows she is a child of God and that makes her unique in His eyes, if not in anyone else's.

Beverly knew every word in those journals, but she would not let her past be a stronghold over her future.

She's living the life that even she didn't think she would have or deserved. But God has given her everything that she has, and she is grateful for His love and favor in her life.

The next morning Beverly made a call to her lawyer, a call she made every time she had to travel making sure that if anything happened to her Beverly's daughter would have power of attorney over her estate.

She knew without a doubt that Anita and Amber had to be included in all her plans as well.

Ryan assured her that everything was in order, he also said, "Bev, you know you're God's favorite, and you'll be fine. We'll talk when you return, have a safe trip." She hung up the phone knowing he was right; she was God's child for sure.

After that phone call, she went back to finishing up her packing. Then made some phone calls to her children informing them about this trip on Thursday to Dallas. They had small talk together, but they were busy.

She told them she loved them and would talk again once she landed in Dallas.

They returned their love and wished her a safe trip and whatever she was about to encounter they knew it would be successful. Beverly loved heartfelt talks with her children especially when she could speak with her children all at the same time.

The next few days were busy ones for both Johnathan and Beverly. They each held staff meetings informing them they would be out of town for an indefinite amount of time.

If any serious problems arose while they were gone, they were to contact Mr. White, a board member and he would handle things promptly. If we could not be contacted in an emergency, Mr. White would be the person to contact.

Johnathan called Beverly to ask if she'd like to get something to eat before leaving the job later, we can meet you in an hour is that good for you?" She replied, "yes, I'll meet you downstairs in an hour."

They went to one of her favorite restaurants. The dinner was great, and so was the company, as always. Johnathan is witty, and not as intense when he's out of the office.

"Thanks for this treat John, I guess we should be leaving because we have to get up extremely early tomorrow." Beverly stated. Johnathan smiled, "Bev, be ready by 5:30 a.m. so we can head out early because you know that airport is always busy no matter what time of day it is." Beverly saluted him jokingly. They walked back to the office parking lot then he walked her to her car and watched her as she drove off.

Johnathan walked to his car parked across the street and sat there thinking to himself *would he ever get a real date with Ms. Jensen or would it always be business as usual?*

He wondered if she even knew that he might be attracted to her. They enjoyed each other's company when they were together.

Johnathan put his key in the ignition and proceeded to the highway heading home for another night alone. As Beverly got closer to her home, she thought; *would Mr. Sheppard ever ask her out for a date again? She had turned him down a few years ago because she wouldn't mix business with pleasure.*

She needed to keep things in perspective; this is what Beverly kept telling herself. Whenever they were in each other's company, he made her feel special like there wasn't anyone else in the room but her.

She thought, isn't that the way a man should make a woman feel? The car behind her honked his horn, and she realized that she had been daydreaming again.

By the time she reached her house and walked inside her luggage was sitting by the door. Anita and Amber finished packing her things so she would be ready and on time the next morning. *"How sweet"*, she thought.

She smiled and thought to herself, *I love these guys.* She'd leave them a note of thanks before leaving in the morning, but for now, she just wanted to sleep so she could be fresh and awake at that early hour tomorrow.

Bev was thankful for this day and said her prayers, showered and slipped into the bed, knowing that 5 a.m. would come quickly. As she rested her head on the pillow, *she was still thinking about Johnathan and wondered if he would...*

The next morning Anita was up when Beverly came downstairs. Sis, why are you up at this crazy hour? Go back to bed Beverly whispered. Excuse me, Ms. Jensen laughing and yawning at the same time. "I wanted to pray with you and Johnny before you guys left. Amber wrote you a note wishing you safe travel.

Read it please, asked Bev" Anita said, "no Sis read it yourself." Beverly grabbed a cup of green tea and one of Anita's homemade zucchini muffins that she loved and put one on a plate for Johnathan.

Anita heard the car pull up and the door open. "Hello," Johnathan called out. Both ladies motioned to him, come in and just grabbed his hand so they could all pray together. Johnathan accepted the muffin and tea when Beverly said, we should be leaving and thanked Anita for the prayer and the breakfast. Love you Sis. Then they left for the airport.

At the airport, the procedure went smoothly, and within a short time, they were about to board the plane to Dallas. The flight was surprisingly pleasant, and the weather was clear even if there were two layovers.

Beverly took the window seat and decided to get some rest and Johnathan was reading the reports he received from his assistant. Beverly glanced over at Johnathan and sighed shaking her head knowing that he should be taking a nap too.

But she knew he was a work-a-holic, that's all he did was work and think about work. *God bless him,* she thought then she closed her eyes.

It was close to 2 p.m. before they had their first layover in St. Louis, MO. It was cloudy but warm, so Johnathan decided to browse the Mall since they had two hours to spare. He asked, Bev, to accompany him, and she agreed. She didn't want to shop just browse.

So, they browsed for an hour and grabbed a bite to eat before boarding the next plane to Dallas. Once seated she decided to take another nap because she felt exhausted.

After an hour, Johnathan glanced over at her and smiled

to himself. He thought *she looked so peaceful sleeping.* He bent over and kissed her forehead. Beverly felt the light kiss but never opened her eyes, she *was thinking, "that's so sweet."* Finally arriving at the Dallas airport, it was close to 11:30 p.m., when Johnathan and Beverly reached the hotel, they said good night went to their separate suites and went to bed.

They both had messages from their assistants the next morning informing them that they had two meetings in the morning, with the C.E.O.'s. The Convention Center is on the outskirts of Dallas in the business section of the city. The morning was sweltering, nearly 95 degrees, and it was only 8:30 am.

They walked up to the building they keep stopping and glancing at each other because the building didn't appear like a Convention Center from the outside. But surprised once inside, the inside was much better than the outside, looks are deceiving. The furniture was semi-modern, the meeting sections had big heavy Texan style furnishings. Beverly wasn't surprised in the least. Ten-gallon hats and bull horns were decorating the walls. After all the meetings and leadership sessions ended Beverly was so ready to head back home.

On the way back to the airport Beverly noticed there were several messages from Erika Brownstone's office regarding another emergency meeting.

New York City seemed like a long way home at this

moment to Beverly. But she was thinking about the meeting they encountered before leaving for the Conference and what impact it will have on the headquarters office back home.

She was hoping that once the investigation began for the Manhattan office that they wouldn't find any fraud or any other thing that would indicate mismanagement of funds and policy practices.

This would force the main office to take extreme measures to correct and maintain respect for the workers. Were the executives in these offices hiding something?

She had so many questions running around in her head that she felt a nap might be what she needed to do to dismiss all the things running through her mind. She was sure Johnathan had the same concerns.

Johnathan would call a full board meeting when they returned because the reports that they reviewed and the reports that he received were not matching up, highlighting some serious concerns for both offices.

Beverly also had something else to contemplate, her next meeting with Ms. Brownstone regarding her promotion and relocating to Arizona or Washington. She'd been praying for a clear answer, but as of now she still hadn't gotten what she felt was a sure answer from the Holy Spirit.

She had spoken to Johnathan about the move, and he wasn't sure he was willing to leave either. What they both believed was that God is in charge and whatever the outcome, "He'll get the Glory."

Johnathan and Beverly were aware that the main office had been quietly monitoring the Manhattan office for some months now.

They just hadn't been able to send anyone worthy of handling the managers, until Johnathan sent his best team out there. Maybe Johnathan and Beverly have a unique talent of how to deal with the executives.

Reports had been questioned before, but the issues could never be pinpointed. The directors would have lengthy phone conversations with the executives but never getting clear and definitive answers.

So now that Johnathan and Beverly have compared reports regarding the results, the main office will be handling them differently than before. Once the meeting was arranged for them to meet with Ms. Brownstone, they were not surprised to see that two of the Board members and the managers Johnathan had sent to the Manhattan office were also at this meeting.

Two board members Mr. White and Ms. Teasdale came to compare the reports from a couple of months ago and the recent reports given to Johnathan did not match up which could affect their funding.

Mrs. Brownstone informed her two executives that they would not have anything further to do with these reports which would be transferred to the proper divisions, to complete the investigations.

She thanked them for following up without delay and acknowledged and appreciated them for their diligent work. She knew the company may have never gotten down to the bottom of this issue without their help.

"Ms. Jensen, would like to discuss your next meeting for the promotion and relocation?"

Beverly glanced over at Johnathan and then back at

Erika and responded. "Well Mrs. Brownstone I know my thirty days had been pushed back due to this emergency meeting and truthfully, I haven't made a decision. I'm sure by the time next meeting I'll have an answer."

Mr. Sheppard, do you have anything you'd like to discuss regarding this situation?" Johnathan said, "Yes I do, but not today."

Mrs. Brownstone said, "Well, I'm sure that you both are ready to sleep in your own beds tonight you both had a long flight." They both smiled and replied, "Yes we are Mrs. Brownstone."

"Well again thank you for everything and please take tomorrow off and just regroup, don't you agree Mr. White and Ms. Teasdale?" They both responded unanimously, "Yes, please on the company."

Beverly and Johnathan walked out of Ms. Brownstone's office to the elevators and exited out the building by then the sun was setting delivering a fantastic array of beautiful colors in the sky.

Johnathan asked Beverly if she would consider grabbing a bite to eat. Beverly declined and told John that she just wanted to go to her house and check on her family. "Beverly, are you trying to avoid me?" NO! why would you ever think that, I just want to go home."

Johnathan understood although he was hoping to spend more time with her. OK, he said, walking her to her car and waiting until she strapped the seatbelt on before he reminded her, "I'll call and check on you later."

His car was parked next to hers; he leaned over and gave her a kiss that was supposed to be an innocent kiss on her cheek but ended up being a very intimate kiss, then he got in his car and headed for the highway.

Beverly daydreamed about that kiss all the way home. Before Beverly could get out of the car, Johnathan pulled up behind her and was heading for her car.

He opened her door and got inside, and she looked surprised, he leaned over and kissed her for several minutes before allowing her to say a word. Finally, she pulled back to look at him and kissed him even deeper this time and then rushed out of the car without even looking back or saying anything to Johnathan.

He got back in his car and drove to his house, smiling all the way there. Beverly rushed into her house without looking behind her to see if he was looking or had left. She did hear the car pull off after a few minutes once she was inside. She realized she just acted like a teenager, not a grown woman.

Amber walked into the living room and hugged her Aunt. "Auntie I missed you, it's been six whole days," Beverly smiled and hugged her back and admittingly agreed, "Yes, Amber I know; I missed you and your mom too by the way, where is she?" "Oh Mom, she's still working, she catered a big office anniversary tonight; she'll probably be in late again." "Again?" Beverly questioned. "Yeah she's been working every evening since you left the last week."

"That's great, Beverly stated, I'm happy for her she

wants to get as many customers as possible to have a good customer base when she opens her restaurant."

Auntie, does that mean she'll be working late hours when she opens her business? Beverly answered, probably, but you'll be there helping her, won't you?

"Yes, I'll be there every chance I get." "Well, I'm sure she'll appreciate any time you can help her."

"Amber I'd love to talk, but I need to shower, and I need rest and relaxation. When I'm done, you're welcome to come and climb in my bed, and we'll talk until one of us falls asleep," she chuckled.

Amber laughed and told her, "I think you should shower, climb into your bed and sleep, until tomorrow morning when you have to get ready for work." Beverly laughed, guess what Amber, I don't have to go into the office tomorrow so we can hang out. "Good night."

Beverly tried to lay down, but there was so much going on in her head until she finally got up went downstairs and made herself a cup of chamomile tea. This would allow her mind to slow down enough to get some sleep and after about thirty minutes Beverly was sound asleep.

Amber peeped in on Beverly, but she was sound asleep, so she shut the door and went to her room. Anita was just getting in the door. Amber turned around and went downstairs to let her mom know Auntie Bev was home but she went straight to bed she was tired Mom

Anita said, "I'm glad she's back home safe. I knew after a week out there in Texas, she would be exhausted. Next thing Amber said was, by the way she's off tomorrow I was wondering if you were off too? I would love to have a family day together, wouldn't you Mom?" "Yes, Amber I would and as far as I know I don't have any early appointments either."

"So, unless Bev has something urgent to do tomorrow, I guess the family day is on." Anita stated.

"Mom, you know I love you both." "We love you more baby girl." When are you going to stop calling me baby girl, I'm 20 years old?" Anita smiled and carefully explained," Come here, missy" she hugged Amber and said, "You'll always be my "Baby Girl" even when your 65!" "Okay, Okay! Mom you win."

Anita heading for the kitchen, "Hey hon, I'm making some tea want some?" "I'm running upstairs, I'll be right back." Amber was still talking about tomorrow as she headed upstairs. "Mom I have a great idea! tomorrow we can grill in the backyard and pick some apples off the tree for your great apple tarts.

The next morning Beverly laid in her bed until 11 a.m. which was highly unusual for her.

Amber and Anita didn't want to disturb her, so they fixed a small breakfast and put some aside for her later. Around noon Beverly finally came downstairs.

Anita heard her in the kitchen and walked in surprised, "Sis, what's up girl, you must have been exhausted because I don't remember the last time you slept this late girl." Beverly responded, "I know, so glad to be back home sleeping in my bed." "There's no place like home." Anita said, "I know that's right." The ladies enjoyed their long weekend and they did a plethora of things the entire time.

Beverly had to make a crucial decision regarding accepting the new position by the next meeting with

Ms. Brownstone which had been pushed back due to the emergency meetings, the audits, the Conference in Texas. The whole thing was starting to become stressful.

One thing Beverly was sure about was that if this meeting went well and she accepted the position as CEO for the Washington office she would not be leaving New York without Anita and Amber.

Beverly decided to do some research on Washington because she didn't know too much about that state. She was aware that it was a large steelworker state back in the day, but how was the economy today? How was the job market? the living conditions? the education? etc. All this information must be factored into her decision.

Erika promised to give her the full layout of the business plans for this new project when and if she accepted the position.

Well, it's Tuesday and the week is already off to an interesting one.

Her co-workers are stopping by her office with small talk about anything and everything, but what they really want to know is if Beverly will be accepting this new position.

Beverly didn't discuss her first meeting with Ms. Brownstone with anyone except Anita and her Pastor. Until the next meeting and a decision is made, all talks are on hold, they'll just have to wait and see.

Well, the busyness of the week resulted in Beverly not being able to concentrate on the upcoming meeting and, before she realized it, the meeting was just a day away. The next morning Beverly reviewed the status reports and made some business calls.

Beverly's assistant made some arrangements for some policy staff meeting with the managers next week also.

At approximately 5:30 p.m., Carol informed Beverly that Jennifer who was Ms. Brownstone's assistant had called and the meeting was pushed back until 6:00 p.m. because some emergencies had come up without notice of course as emergencies usually do.

Beverly thanked Carol and went to her bathroom in her office to check her makeup and made sure her stockings weren't twisted. *Twisted stockings are the worst thing that could happen she thought.*

At the appointed time Beverly left her office and took the elevator up to the C.E.O.'s office feeling confident and smiling not anxious like was the first time she visited the 32nd floor.

Ms. Brownstone gestured for her to take a seat because she was on a business call, she smiled and held up her hand to indicate five minutes more. Beverly shook her head and smiled back indicating she understood. The call sounded quite intense, and Beverly felt a little uncomfortable, but Erika turned her back, so Beverly just sat down.

The phone call ended, and Erika extended her apologies to Beverly for the lengthy phone call, of course Beverly smiled and told her it was alright, "Business is Business."

Ms. Brownstone offered her something to drink, but Beverly declined. After that, she suggested, "well let's get down to the business at hand, Ms. Jensen."

She asked, Beverly, if she had considered the offer on the table and if she did accept then another meeting would be arranged to explain what the position entailed, it was final that Washington was the new location instead of Arizona.

Beverly spoke clearly and looked directly at Erika and said, "after much prayer conversation with my family, I have decided to accept the position.

She expressed her gratitude for Beverly's decision. Fully aware that Ms. Jensen had made the right choice.

Beverly expressed that this opportunity would be beneficial to her and thousands of people in the Washington area. She expressed feeling confident of handling this new venture and how excited she was to discuss her ideas for the programs."

Ms. Brownstone listened carefully watching Beverly's body language and thought to herself, *"This woman is going to be a powerhouse as the new C.E.O."*

Beverly had the confidence that made her a good leader.

Erika recognized the sincerity in what Beverly was saying and the excitement in her voice.

This was an opportunity for Beverly to help people less fortunate and that was something she loved about working in this capacity.

Ms. Brownstone and Ms. Jensen had a visual media meeting with the executive staff in the Washington office. Introducing Ms. Jensen to that staff and making them aware that she will be the new C.E.O. coming on board soon. As Beverly glanced around the screen, she noticed that it was a mixed group. Three Afro-American women, two Chinese women, three Afro-American gentlemen, and two Caucasian men.

Beverly felt comfortable she could work with anyone and has always been able to for many years. She liked her new teams so far as they discussed their individual staff responsibilities and hoped that Ms. Jensen would bring her own new ideas to the staff. They were all looking forward to working with her soon.

The next meeting was with the Board of Directors which was a conference call which went very well indeed. Ms. Brownstone assured Beverly that both teams will be behind her 100%.

So, Erika suggested that they go to lunch with their teams and celebrate the new beginnings and the new position. Beverly believed this opportunity as a new beginning.

Beverly agreed to meet Erika and their people for this luncheon, but first, she needed to clean up her desk downstairs and make a couple of important calls to some of her managers. They both agreed to meet in an hour, and Ms. Brownstone insisted on treating Beverly and her team.

She was feeling overwhelmed and blessed. Beverly said, "thank you so much" and hugged Erika and said, "thank you again."

Erika gently pushed Beverly toward the door saying, "We only have an hour before we meet up Ms. Jensen, so please leave now, and I'll see you in an hour." "Yes, we will."

As Beverly entered the elevator, she whispered a quick prayer and praised the Holy Spirit for His handy work in this endeavor, as in everything that He has blessed her with.

Once downstairs, Beverly's first call was to her Pastor to tell her the good news. They spoke for a short time and then hung-up. The next call was to Anita who knew immediately what the call was about due to the excitement in Bev's voice.

This call was short also, and they agreed to speak later but what Beverly didn't know is that the same people she just talked to would see her in an hour.

They had been invited to the luncheon by Erika's assistant a week ago in anticipation of Beverly decision to accept the offer of CEO.

Beverly made some more calls than glanced out the window recalling that this had been a long, tough journey, one that caused her to bust her butt to get to this very place at this time in her life.

It's a place of achievement, and she felt truly blessed for this incredibly special day. She knew that her sister-friend would be excited and would celebrate with her for this new blessing.

The difficult issue was that she would be leaving her Pastor, her church family and Assistant Pastor N. Cherry who had counseled her through many of her difficult situations over the years. They were her rock when she felt like giving up. She had been under the wings and wisdom of Pastor D. E. Wright and Associate Pastor N. Cherry, her spiritual leaders who have prayed her through her hurdles.

They were always available to help her understand how to get intimate with the Spirit of the Living God. God always brings you the people that you need when we accept that we need His guidance.

When we begin to seek His love and Word, we prosper

not only financially but in other ways that prove "God is real." Pastor D. E. Wright's teaching will take her anywhere in the world because she knows who she is and whose she is. Beverly had discussed this offer with her Pastor when she was first asked to take the position, and they prayed for clarity before Bev made her final decision.

Beverly also contacted her children to plan a group dinner to let them know her decision about accepting her new position.

She is going to be shocked when she arrives at this luncheon, to see her children there. The company flew them in, and they were staying at a hotel near the office.

Even though her children are older and living their lives, she loved them dearly and kept them abreast of all her endeavors, and they did the same with her. Beverly knew that there would be so much of the city that she'd miss, thinking to herself, *New York will always be home.*

Beverly checked her pager to see Anita left a message letting her know that she would be out for most of the afternoon. Anita didn't want to give the surprise away. The message also stated, Sis I'm so proud of you.

It was close to the time to meet Erika for this luncheon, and she didn't know who else would be there, so she went to freshen up before heading downstairs to the lobby.

When Beverly stepped out of the elevator, she was shocked there was a crowd of her co-workers holding flowers, smiling, and clapping, shocked she said, "Oh my goodness!"

Beverly thought, *Erika had set her up.* How did all these folks know what the outcome of this meeting would be?

Was everyone else so sure that she would accept this new position before she did? Beverly was smiling because she always knew news traveled around the office fast.

What Beverly didn't know was that Ms. Brownstone had arranged reservations at a swanky restaurant. Beverly was blown away by the gratitude and appreciation being displayed for the work she's done all these years with this company.

After being seated in the section reserved for this group, which included Anita, Amber along with people that Beverly had worked with over the years, the highlight was when her children walked into the restaurant; this brought her to tears of joy. They hugged her then went and sat with Anita and Amber.

Patting her eyes so as not to mess up her makeup, Beverly began walking around networking with her co- workers. People were asking her so many questions, and she began to feel overwhelmed.

After about fifteen minutes of networking, Erika asked people to be seated. Erika took a deep breath to clear her head and asked everyone for their attention. Everyone stopped talking amongst themselves and turned their attention toward Erika.

She started by thanking everyone for attending the luncheon. "We're all here to celebrate Ms. Beverly Jensen on accepting her new position as CEO in our new division in Washington."

"I'm proud that after many months of deliberation with the Board of Directors of both divisions we feel our choice was the best. Ms. Jensen has proven to be a dedicated, reliable, hardworking individual. She has worked long and hard to move up the corporate ladder as many of you are aware."

"Ms. Beverly Jensen has given more of herself than many expected her to do, also she has been instrumental in implementing our most rewarding programs for our youth, preparing many of them to step into jobs in companies that they may have never been able to without her direction and training skills."

Then Erika introduced Ms. Jensen to the group and asked her to say a few words.

Beverly stepped up to the podium and said, "First and foremost I have to thank My Lord and Savior, people starting clapping.

Beverly held up her hand Without God, we cannot do anything, but I'm not here to preach my friends, I'm here today to thank you for taking out time from your busy schedules to come and celebrate this important milestone in my life.

"It's been many years of hard work and sacrifice, as Ms. Brownstone mentioned but it has all been worth it. For this day, this time in my life, I'm about to take a position that requires a high level of diligence and faith. I didn't believe it at first myself. But, the Word of God says, "He knows the plans that He has for our lives."

"I'm grateful that I have been chosen to begin this new program in a city whose young people are crying for help. I'm hoping that we will encourage, foster and facilitate positivity in each young person that will enter our building in search of training and a better future.

"What I'm asking of each and every one of you sitting here today is that we pray for each other.

"There are many folks here today that know the pitfalls we experience during the initial startup period of any new endeavor, so I'm hoping that everyone allows me to reach out to you when I need some encouragement and assistance.

"I feel confident that this endeavor is one in God's plans, I want everyone to know I'm not that far away and I'm hoping that at any time you need advice remember that I'm just a phone call away.

"I also hope that goes both ways. Most of us have been with this company for some 20 plus years, so we're like family. We watched our babies grow up, we celebrated marriages and cried over the loss of loved ones.

"So, again I say from the bottom of my heart, thank you for all these memories, and may God bless each and every one of you here today.

"I want to acknowledge and thank the Board of Directors for giving me this opportunity. Being a new CEO in a new state is a challenge I genuinely believe we are a little nervous but also enthusiastic about it all at the same time. I have a great team working with me and I believe we can be as successful there as we have been here.

Oh, please, don't let me forget to thank the great staff that I have worked with for many years. I'll miss you all, but I have no doubt that the great programs we established will continue to thrive due to the dedication that everyone has continued to show over the years."

Beverly glanced over at Erika indicating, that she's just

about finished with her speech. People were wiping their eyes and clapping at the same time.

Ms. Brownstone stood up then sat back down looking a little weary. Then she stood up again and said. "I think we've said enough, let's eat." Everyone clapped and was shaking their heads in agreement.

Beverly didn't want to bring people to tears, but she was passionate about letting them know how blessed and grateful she felt, especially being able to work with young people which has always been something close to her heart. By this time, the food was arriving the group were laughing and networking again, then Beverly asked her Pastor to pray over the food.

The food was fabulously tasty, and they offered a large selection. This was one of Beverly's favorite restaurants in this area. Beverly's children waved, so she went and sat with them, she was so glad to see all her children together.

Then she noticed Johnathan talking to Erika. He glanced over her way and winked at her. She had mixed feelings toward Johnathan. He was handsome and still single as far as she knew, and he was also a top executive in the company.

Johnathan had attempted to talk with her on a personal level, but she was always consumed by work and never made time for dating, although, she had him over to her house several times for cookouts and dinners.

What Beverly wasn't aware of was that Johnathan would also be going to this new business venture with her. Erika hadn't mentioned this to her yet.

Johnathan walked over to where Beverly was seated and

he kissed her on the cheek and congratulated her on her very impressive promotion. He was happy to see her family, her children had met Johnathan years ago.

He also asked if they could have dinner together before she left town. She smiled and said, "I think that could be something I'd consider."

The staff, family, and friends stayed about an hour and a half at the restaurant one the people started leaving.

Erika asked the remaining staff to moved to the smaller location in the restaurant she reserved to hold a meeting with the Board of Directors that had traveled from the other offices. Erika thought it would be nice to hold a meeting outside the confines of an office building.

Now Beverly, Erika, and Johnathan, with the other nine Board members and the executives sat down to discuss the final details of the plans and what they expected from the team that would be heading up this program.

Carol had brought her portfolio and the ideas that the architects had developed with her. Everyone brought their ideas also. This meeting allowed everyone to collaborate their ideas for this new division.

The company was offering a nice severance package for the transfer that included paying her mortgage for the first four months until the new company was fully up and running smoothly.

This offer would make the transition seem much easier to accept. Beverly planned to convince Anita and Amber to relocate with her, and she hoped Anita would consider.

Johnathan or Mr. Sheppard as he was addressed displayed a miniature scale of the building the company architects had designed which included a large parking lot, a gym, and a new youth service center which would in include housing vouchers for homeless youth and young mothers in-house services like babysitting, job training, and many other services. As well as a shopping Mall that is not yet completed.

Beverly must have had a look of amazement on her face because both Erika and Johnathan smiled at her when he started speaking about this project. Johnathan and Beverly would be allowed to select which stores would do well in the Mall.

The designing of the complex completely depended on how they wanted its accessibility to the service division, separate from the Mall. This would require spending time with their architects. Both were capable of this task plus the Board knew they would work well together.

So, when Carol opened the portfolio, she presented the architects ideas that they had worked on for months. This was the designs for the upcoming Mall. Everyone was amazed at the details of this small-scale model. They weren't quite ready for this, but of course Beverly was on point with her demonstration.

Beverly began realizing that this was no small project, not if it consists of a small shopping center that is waiting for her approval. There were a couple of millions of dollars involved in the project.

Erika didn't quite tell her all this was involved. But she's sure she can handle it. Once the designs were completed there will be a meeting with the building managers at the new location. This presentation went very well.

Johnathan and Beverly will be flying out to oversee the projects making sure things go smoothly and are completed on time or at least close to the deadline.

Beverly was fully aware that time would become intense, and the weeks were going by quickly. Beverly was so busy putting things in order before they traveled. Ms. Brownstone released Beverly and Johnathan from their present assignments and started to distribute them to other managers and staff in their divisions.

Beverly was relieved for that because it allowed her to focus on the matter at hand as her new project needed her full attention. She didn't want any mistakes and most importantly didn't want to waste any of the allotted funds.

Johnathan and Beverly started working closer, as the time got closer to fly out to Washington.

Beverly was impressed with his work ethic; he was professional and knowledgeable about both ventures which meant he did his homework, as she had also done.

They had several weekly conference calls with the construction crew, and things seemed to be coming together without a glitch.

Meanwhile, bids were being submitted from different stores hoping for an approval for a spot in the new upcoming Mall. Beverly handed her files to Carol, picked her bags up and glanced around her office to make sure she had cleared off her desk.

She went to press the elevator button, but Erika called out to her as she was stepping into the elevator, which was surprising, Erika on her floor, *this must be important*, she thought.

She just wanted to go home, but duty calls, at least as far as she knew, in her position it would always be that way. So, Beverly waved to Erika and silently prayed it wasn't more bad news.

The length of the hallway was rather long, so Beverly decided to sit in one of the comfortable chairs by the elevator to wait for Erika to reach her.

When Erika did finally reach her Beverly was curious to see what Erika was carrying in her hand. Erika sat down and opened the folder containing papers and she handed them to Beverly.

Beverly looked them over and was amazed at what she saw.

Two major companies had bid the highest, and they would bring in top revenues for the Mall. Now Beverly was also smiling and said, "Praise the Lord." Was this the calm before the storm?

Even though Erika wasn't much of a churchgoer, she fully agreed with Beverly on this one. Just then Johnathan came out of the other elevator and glanced at them as he was stepping off.

Erika had asked him to meet with her and Beverly before they left the building. They asked him to take a glance at the reports, and he too was surprised at what he saw. Things were looking good. Even though some problems had arisen, Erika felt that the project would continue, and everything would be alright. Beverly looked at Erika and wondered how she was feeling; she was looking a little pale. When Beverly asked her, she responded by saying "Oh I feel like I'm coming down with a cold or something, I'll be fine, thanks for asking."

Erika was so pleased with these results she invited them both for dinner and drinks on her. They both wanted to decline, but that would have been rude besides how often do you get to sit down with the C.E.O? So, they agreed, and Erika told them, "I'll meet you in the lobby in ten minutes, let me get my bags and inform Jennifer." They told Erika they would meet her at the restaurant, and she agreed and left.

Beverly and Johnathan decided that they would walk to the restaurant together giving them a little time to talk about the reports before meeting with Erika.

Situation can change drastically within days and although nobody wished for anything close to a disaster to happen, well into the fifth month, all these elements had hit these construction sites. This meant that all construction work and the workers had to stop immediately. First, a horrendous rainstorm that lasted two weeks straight with winds close to 45 mph, and a few days later three pipes burst to flood the entire first floor of the buildings.

After that Washington had another problem, 37 inches

of snow, leaving many people stranded without a way to get home. One of the worst snowstorms they had experienced since 1963.

Neither Johnathan nor Beverly got upset because they were smart enough to know there's nothing, they could have done to prevent this. So, they just went with the flow and said, "This too shall pass, Amen, and thank you, Lord."

The weather was getting cold, and soon it would be snowing which meant that the work would have to be close to being completed before the heavy snowstorms. There are always elements that can shut down any outdoor construction project. Rain, windstorms, hurricanes, ice, and power outages or water pipe bursting.

They were not in the midst of this plan because it could have been worse. We may be the C.E.O.'s, but they both agree that God is in charge. Hopefully, by the time Bev and Johnathan were planning to travel, the plan had been pushed back to allow some time for the workers to see if it's possible to salvage the site.

This was the perfect opportunity while walking to the restaurant for Beverly to ask Johnathan if he'd like to attend the concert at her church on Sunday. He smiled and said he'd be delighted to go with her and her family.

The weekend was coming around again, and Beverly was

hoping to run into Johnathan before he left the building to invite him to her church.

They were having a concert and a dinner afterward and thought maybe he'd enjoy that since she felt he knew the Lord and also it would be nice to see him somewhere other than work but she didn't want to send the wrong message.

He asked if he could pick her up, but she thought about it and wondered what the church family might think, but she decided that she would allow him to escort her on Sunday anyway. They agreed to meet at ten o'clock; *this was a great idea,* she thought to herself.

The dinner was relaxing, and the company was good also. However, they didn't talk shop, which made the evening enjoyable for everyone.

While having their coffee Johnathan's beeper vibrated, at first it seemed he didn't want to answer it.

Johnathan excused himself and walked away from the table. When he returned, Beverly asked if everything was okay? He didn't say much except his mom had been admitted into the hospital again, and I'm going to meet up with my sister later.

We were expecting Johnathan to excuse himself and leave, but he just sat down and resumed the conversation.

After dinner and drinks were over, everyone shared hugs and started to walk toward their cars. Erika had driven because she had to meet her hubby, so she said her goodbyes and left just before they did.

Beverly didn't want to pry, but she asked him was there something going on with his Mother that he wanted to talk about?

Johnathan looked at Bev and said, "No I'm going to meet up with my sister at her place and get the details."

Then he walked out of the restaurant with her. It didn't seem like he wanted to talk about this matter at all. "Oh, I guess I won't see you Sunday then due to this family issue?"

But he stopped, he smiled at her with the raised eyebrow look and said, "Bev, I'll pick you up at 10 a.m. on Sunday, have a nice weekend, until then." Beverly didn't know how to reply, so she just said, "Alright see you then have a good weekend too, hope everything goes well."

Erika sat in her car thinking about what had just occurred. Johnathan had worked for the company longer than she had in his division, but she never knew whether he had family or not.

In fact, she realized that she didn't know too much about any of the other executives or managers. That's something she would have to look into more.

As Beverly was just about to pull off her beeper rang, she looked at the beeper to see it was Amber. Beverly had forgotten to call her to let her know she was alright and just hanging out with the bosses. Beverly returned to the office and called Amber.

Beverly asked her if they were coming over to the house, "Auntie we're at your place already." "Oh, good that's great!" Beverly said. "Auntie, Mom, didn't feel well, she went upstairs to lay down." "I'll be there soon Amber. "Amber told her she was starting to get a tad bit worried.

The weekend had begun in a somewhat puzzling manner and Beverly was concerned about her friend. She also thought about Johnathan's mother, but enough of trying to figure that one out, as usual she was overthinking. She believed in his time he would explain the details, or would he?

Beverly, like Erika, had worked with Johnathan for several years now but didn't know too much about his personal life except that he had a twin sister, and both were single, but his Mother was never a part of his conversations.

Now Beverly was pulling into her garage and she didn't want to be bogged down with the office problems she wanted to concentrate on some serious relaxation, everything else would have to wait. She didn't even want to talk on the phone anymore this evening.

Even though Beverly wanted to relax she could not stop thinking about this Johnathan situation, and why he never mentioned his family.

Was there something he was ashamed of that he didn't want his staff or her to know or was it that he didn't want to mix his personal business with work?

Beverly just wondered to herself because she never wanted to be nosy, but Johnathan was her friend, and this was really beginning to bother her. She decided to pray on whatever he was facing and let it go.

Before getting in her bed, she got on her knees and prayed for everyone in her life and thanked her God for blessings, grace and mercy than she climbed into her bed for a good night's sleep after such a hectic work week - this was what she looked forward to.

Beverly believed that the Holy Spirit continued to open opportunities for her because she tried to live a Christian life and whenever her Pastor requested her services, she had never forgotten that she was just a servant of the Lord, first and foremost. So, she thanked Him, and she repented every night for sins known and unknown.

Something Beverly learned from her years of attending church and getting intimate with her God and reading the Scriptures, was that she or we cannot do anything without believing that we are led by the Spirit and through obedience we receive our blessings.

Her faith has taken her through many difficult and dark times in her life. She often lays in her bed tearful when she remembers her past and how the Lord brought her through every valley situation so she can only praise Him every chance she gets.

Based on how her life began, she would have never thought she would ever be given the opportunity to become a C.E.O. of a Fortune 500 company, with all the amenities and more money than she could have ever thought of making in her lifetime.

Beverly is extremely grateful for God's grace and mercy. God gives us unconditional love, grace, and mercy daily. Beverly was thinking about *when she first met Anita and Amber and how they have been a blessing in her life. She remembered the day Anita gave her life to Christ and how they rejoiced, and she drifted off to sleep.*

After a good night's sleep, the morning routine as usual was Bev going to the kitchen for a smoothie and then downstairs for some exercise. When she got there, she found Anita already on the treadmill.

Bev said, "girl, you beat me! I must have really been tired, sis." Anita laughed and said, "You better catch up girlfriend," they both laughed.

After exercising Anita explained to Beverly her lease was about to end and she couldn't afford to pay the higher rent.

Not with the tuition payments for Amber's college. Anita's deceased husband David had left them well off to a degree.

Beverly's responded with, "Why are you worrying, don't you know I got your back girlfriend?" "You already know upstairs will always be your place so pack whatever you have left and finish moving completely in Anita…. End of discussion."

Hey, whatever furniture you don't want upstairs put in storage in the back of the house just in case you decide to move out later."

"Now, that problem is solved because it was never a problem to begin with, right Anita," "Yes Sis it is," Anita answered with a smile.

Anita already knew it in her heart that Beverly always wanted them to move in after learning about the nightmares Anita was experiencing. This was a double blessing for both ladies.

Anita smiled and said, "OK Captain"! Beverly suggested, Sis if you need the movers to get the rest of your furniture in, their number is in the Rolodex in the kitchen, I'll give them a heads up letting them know my sister needs them, so we'll have the furniture moved in ASAP. It's difficult trying to live in two places when we don't have to, Anita said, "I know I can always count on you, love you, Sis." "Ditto Sis."

Anita aspired to start a catering business in which she allowed culinary students to work and earn income. Anita would be saving money and Anita the chef would cook most of their meals. Yes, Beverly thought, *that's what I'm talking about.* They slapped each other high five,

They also talked about Johnathan's strange action after his phone call from his sister, the sister that they hadn't heard about in years.

But Johnathan's Mom is in the hospital, he never really spoke about her, has he?"

"No Sis not that I can remember off hand", Beverly said. Strange though at least that's how we felt because Erika seemed to look bewildered when she heard him say it too.

Beverly shrugged her shoulders with that questionable look in her face. That was the end of that conversation, for now anyway.

Bev said, since it was cloudy and raining, that she would rather just relax and cook then go into her nothingness mode. Anita said, "Girl I'm feeling the same way, I had a hectic week, too.

By the time the ladies got back upstairs Amber was

in the kitchen attacking the fridge, you know how young people act when they're hungry.

Beverly said, "Hey lady want me to whip up something quick?"

Amber turned around and gave Bev a bear hug and said, "Can't wait we need to get to the store to pick up a few things and hurry back, it's supposed to be a bad rainstorm today."

"Well if that is true then I guess we'd better rush and get dressed and run to the store," Beverly told her. They agreed and started upstairs. The townhouse was three stories.

Amber had the top floor, and Anita had the middle floor and Beverly the lower floor. Amber loved her Aunt Bev's house. Amber was coming back downstairs preparing to go to the store.

Johnathan was sitting in his twin sister's loft apartment waiting for her to get ready to go once again to visit their mother in the hospital's Alzheimer's facility. She had been missing for several days and was found downtown sitting in front of a clothing store.

Johnathan's mother suffers from Alzheimer's, and because of both their busy schedules they decided to have her put in a facility that could provide the care necessary. Until this week they had taken excellent care of her. So, Johnathan and JoAnn were both upset that this happened.

JoAnn was a regular visitor at the facility.

But the week of this incident she had gone on a retreat

and Johnathan was also out of town. Their mother could have been hurt. The staff worker had taken a group of the client's downtown for a field trip.

However, when they got everyone together to return to the facility, their mother was missing from the group. The Police Department was immediately contacted, and the facility managers had also been contacted.

It had taken three days before their mother was located downtown in front of a clothing store, but they wondered where she was during the time she was missing. JoAnn said, "Lord help us, please let our mom be safe."

Up until this incident, they were always thorough with the patients in the facility. So, the twins were quite disturbed when they received this information.

JoAnn was scared for her mother thinking a million things could have happened to her. Her stomach was in knots every time she thought about it. Johnathan didn't express his feelings, but he had prayed for nights without sleep until his mom was located.

JoAnn and Johnathan were twins but had been separated for many years at a young age. Johnathan lived with his paternal grandparents, and JoAnn lived with their mother.

JoAnn was bitter with her brother for many years because she felt he got the better opportunities in his young life.

Although, he did have an enjoyable and interesting childhood, he still had struggles along the way.

He did attend the best private school; he was in the Boy Scouts and the Cadets. He was involved in Church faithfully every Sunday without a choice, of course and also sang in the choir as his grandparents believed every young person needed balance in their life. Johnathan never stopped trying to reach out to his sister.

He would ask his grandparents to buy her new clothes and presents for their birthdays and holidays and they always did. They even went as far as to try and convince his mother to let JoAnn live with them, but she wasn't going to give up her daughter no matter how they tried to assure her JoAnn would be better off with them.

Eventually, JoAnn did wind up staying with them. Her mother developed a serious drug addiction, and JoAnn had witnessed her mother being abused and beaten by men. It destroyed JoAnn and made her more resentful, angry and a complete self- destructive mess.

It was a long time before she shared the tragedies she experienced with her brother and once she did, they began to get closer, and her life was changed ever since.

Now JoAnn was ready to go and see her mother and find out exactly what, if anything, they could do to keep her safe. They were hoping that they wouldn't have to move her again since she had already been moved twice.

This facility had come highly recommended to them by close friends of JoAnn's whose mother had been in this facility for some years now and was very well cared for. During the drive to the Summerset Blvd. Nursing Home, they discussed the best safety measures for their mother. JoAnn's last visit made her realize that her Mother's condition was deteriorating.

This facility had cared for their mother for several years now; however, they had failed? Johnathan agreed, and he was very adamant about it. He was not happy with the current incident and especially because he was about to relocate.

He didn't want his sister having to worry about their mother alone. Johnathan knew he had to always stay in touch for this reason alone.

After they had arrived, they went directly to their mother's room, she was sitting near the window talking to herself about some food on the stove and how it was burning, unfortunately, she didn't acknowledge they were even in the room.

They hugged her, and she looked at them strangely. With Alzheimer's, sometimes she knows her children and sometimes she doesn't.

From day- to- day she could be a different person and at a different place in her mind.

They both noticed their mother's overall health was getting worse, she appeared frail. Johnathan didn't speak to people about his personal life and had been that way most of his adult life because he felt people, would pity him and that was not what he wanted.

So, for him, the fewer people knew, the less he'd have to talk about it.

JoAnn had a support group that she attended weekly to release any feelings she may have about any situation she faced, and it helped her to maintain her life positively. So, both twins found their own way to deal with their problems. Or, had they really?

Johnathan hid his personal life from his friends and JoAnn expressed hers to her support group. But there were things they never disclosed to anyone like most people.

Like Beverly had done for so many years, secrets that nobody wanted to let go of, Johnathan suggested to his sister about returning to church for some spiritual healing that they both needed.

JoAnn still struggled with her past at times, and Johnathan struggled with his guilt of not being around for so many years for his mother and sister, using his work as an excuse. Filling a **VOID**.

They met with the director and discussed their concerns about the recent events. The director was very apologetic and tried to reassure them that this was not something that had happened before, and he wanted them to understand that their mother's care was a priority for him and the staff.

The director had already begun an investigation to see where, if any, did the communication breakdown on the care and security of each resident in this facility.

Johnathan and JoAnn wanted to make sure this was not going to occur again while their mother was in this facility because they had their mother in other places and the care was not professional.

They knew this location was chosen for their quality performance care of patients, so they didn't want to have to remove her, however, would not allow her in any way to be mistreated.

The director explained that she had been escorted outside for a day trip, something they try to incorporate twice monthly so the patients could feel they haven't lost all contact with the outside world.

The nurses in charge stated that another patient was getting ill and they were attending to her, and their mother just didn't stay with the group as everyone was instructed to do and before they knew it, she had walked off. After two days she was found sitting on the bench in front of a dress store.

It just so happened that the store owner recognized that she was acting confused and contacted the authorities.

When the police arrived, she was just sitting in front of the store talking about a dress she had to buy for her daughter's graduation day. She had walked eight blocks from where the group had gathered.

By that time, our head administrator and nurse coordinator were both in the area looking for a few hours hoping to locate your mother. JoAnn reiterated, "thank God she wasn't hurt and was safe when they finally found her."

Johnathan agreed and thanked the director for his time. The director again apologized for this mishap and assured them that he would do everything in his power to make sure it didn't happen again.

Johnathan went back to the room to say goodbye to his mother, and JoAnn followed speaking further with the director. When Johnathan walked into the room, he received a warm greeting from his mom.

"Hi sweetie, your home I'm so glad you got home safe, Johnny." He felt good even though he knew she was living in the past, he walked over to her and hugged and kissed her. Replying, "Yes Mom I'm here."

Once JoAnn entered the room, her mother wasn't sure who she was either but said "Hi sweetie, where were you I wanted you to comb my hair." JoAnn said, sure mom I'll do that now. Her mother's hair had become thin, but it was shoulder length.

JoAnn got the comb and brush and re-braided her hair into another style, although she had just done her hair a few days ago.

After that, her mother spoke in a shallow voice, "I'm tired," and they helped her into her bed for a nap. They both said, "we'll see you later Mom" and left.

They left the facility and walked back to the car, and Johnathan asked his sister what she thought about the director? Well Johnny, "I think he was genuinely concerned didn't you think so Johnny?" He agreed, and they decided to keep their mother in this facility because they had been reassured this incident was handled expeditiously.

Johnathan glanced at his sister for a few minutes, then asked, "Hey what, are you doing later? She answered, "I don't know, why Johnny?"

Only she could call him that. He said, "I thought since we haven't hung out in a while let's go out to dinner or something."

JoAnn smiled saying, "Sure, it has been a while, you need a bonding moment?" Johnathan laughing when she was saying it. Johnathan knew she was teasing him. They had talked via phone, about this big venture and JoAnn was also curious about this move he kept hinting about."

"Alright then I'll be back later. I'll bring something we both like and we'll talk, how's that sis?"

JoAnn grinned and told him that sounds like a great plan, because she knew it was going to be a rainstorm, and she planned on staying inside anyway.

JoAnn dropped her brother back at her place, he walked over to his car and said, "Sis, I'll see you later. Hopefully before the storm." Johnathan had been good to his sister. He bought her a car and helped her move from the broken-down ghetto apartment she lived in into a more decent place away from the drug area that kept her depressed.

JoAnn was grateful for all his help and every time they got together; she always enjoyed his company.

She was looking forward to spending some time with her brother, JoAnn blew him a kiss and said, "See you later, love you, bro."

Johnathan knew that they both were concerned about the care their mother received, and he felt the meeting went well. Johnathan went to the supermarket and picked up dinner for later, he knew they both loved spaghetti so that would be dinner tonight.

Around 6:50 p.m. Johnathan went back to his sister's place, and they enjoyed making dinner together with garlic bread and some sparkling apple cider, since JoAnn was in recovery. They even checked out a funny movie. Spending quality time with her brother made her happy.

This was something they didn't get to do often due to his busy schedule and him always traveling to meetings for the company.

They talked about the amazing new venture that he was about to undertake with Beverly in Washington or Arizona and how much it would help the economy out there. He also wanted his sister to know that if anything happened to their mother, he would fly back immediately. JoAnn told him that hopefully, God will keep her somewhat healthy, but she could tell her health was failing.

The doctor told her she had problems breathing and sleeping at night. They had been giving her a mild sedative to help her rest comfortably.

She also needed oxygen several times during the night. Johnathan said, he knew because the doctor contacted him to get the approval.

He did some research regarding the medication to make sure that it would not have negative effects on what she was already taking. JoAnn then changed the conversation to the business venture that her brother was starting to tell her about. He told her that Beverly would also be running the company in Washington or Arizona. They would be flying in two weeks to see just how the projects were developing.

They had been in constant contact with the contractors, and so far, there had been some glitches, but hopefully, things would work out. Stores had been bidding for spots in the new Mall that's connected with this project.

Well, JoAnn said, "that sounds so exciting, and I'm so proud of you." JoAnn wasn't really a drinker anymore, so she raised her glass of sparkling apple cider that she kept in the fridge. Her brother had bought some wine, so they toasted to his accomplishments.

Johnathan asked his sister what was happening in her

life? She was glad he asked because she had some good news too. JoAnn was now a born-again Christian and had been taking Christian courses through her church. She was also involved in her church's ministries with the girl's group. JoAnn felt good about developing a closer relationship with Christ. This was an achievement for her especially because of her past.

She told her brother that she began attending the women's ministry. JoAnn learned that so many of the woman that attended the church had similar backgrounds. And the only way they felt empowered about themselves was through learning to love themselves and knowing who God was in their lives. This is how the healing began, and they were doing it together. This was a healthy support group for her.

Johnathan noticed it was getting late, so he got up and went over and hugged his sister, told her he was proud of her also and happy that she finally was finding her peace in Christ.

JoAnn asked her brother was he going to help her clean up? Johnathan said, he'd be good and help her clean up before he left. She said she was older, and he had to listen to her. He laughed because she is actually six minutes older." So," he said, "does that make you my boss?" Her answer was "YES it does!"

They went back and forth playfully for a few minutes, like when they were younger.

They laughed so hard they had to catch their breath, and finally, she said, "Alright, bro you win!" but he was already in the kitchen placing the plates in the dishwasher.

They genuinely loved each other because all they had was each other.

Johnathan told his sister he enjoyed spending time together and that they should really try and do this again before he left f. John told his sister that he would be meeting Beverly this weekend to attend a concert at her church.

Sis, you should try and come too. JoAnn smiled and said. "I know you're in love with that woman bro." He didn't say a word which usually meant that she was correct. But he wouldn't admit it either to himself or to Bev. Not yet anyway.

The timing was never right, that was his excuse anyway. JoAnn told her brother that if his schedule was that busy, then he should leave so he could get back to his side of town, it would probably take a good hour or so.

Once in his car, he thought about the conversation he had with his sister regarding Beverly. *He realized that he had deep feelings for this woman, and he wanted to tell her how he felt, but the reality was that it probably wouldn't happen in this lifetime.* Somewhere in the future he really wanted to tell her how he felt but the timing was never quite right.

He recalled the first time he saw her; it was at the company luncheon for Brady, an executive who was retiring. He'd been on the job for forty-something years, so it was time for him to enjoy whatever time he had left, and he was looking forward to that day.

Brady always spoke about traveling to Europe and Greece and countries like that. Retirement should be like that, but not everyone gets that opportunity.

Johnathan was halfway home when the heavens opened up, and the rain started pouring heavily making it difficult to see. Johnathan said, a quick prayer and finally made it safely home, when he arrived at his place, he thanked God for traveling mercies and his sister.

Johnathan sat in his living room and recalled how he felt about Beverly, how graceful she walked and her smile that lit up a room.

He kept those images in his head - her walk, her smile, and her bedroom eyes. How soft her hands were when he was introduced to her through a co-worker and that sweet voice. These were the things he remembered when he thought *of Ms. Beverly Jensen.*

Soon they will be working together on a daily basis and he hoped it would eventually bring them closer than just co-workers. Jonathan called his sister to let her know he had made it home minutes before it poured. "Listen, bro, keep me abreast of how things are going with this new position and venture okay, promise me."

He paused and thought about it, *realizing that he hadn't really kept in touch with his twin sister as much as he should have,* so he promised her that he would get better when it came to calling her and not just when their mother had a problem but really keeping in touch with her.

"Sis, love you, you know, that right?" "Of course, I do Johnny. Have fun with Bev on Sunday." He said, "I'm sure I will. Good night Sis." "'Night Johnny."

Beverly had also been out earlier running some errands, and while she was out, she had planned to meet up with her Pastor who was at the church and Beverly wanted to discuss this move.

Beverly sat in her Pastor's office, and tears started rolling down her face.

Pastor stood up and walked over and just hugged her, finally, Beverly found her composure and sat back down and went through the whole story.

Beverly informed her Pastor that she had accepted the position and she and Johnathan would be going to Washington in about three weeks to meet with the Mayor and the contractors to discuss the plans for this new venture. Arizona wasn't an option any longer.

Her Pastor asked some tough questions regarding the permanent move, and Bev explained that she had mixed feelings. She felt sad because she needed her church family, but at the same time, she was excited about this new experience. She was stepping into a new beginning, and her Pastor understood although she would be greatly missed.

She thanked Beverly for her devotion to God and this ministry for all these years. The Pastor continued saying, "Your dedication has truly been an extraordinary gift that God used to help grow our church, and Beverly you've grown spiritually, and mentally as a woman of God.

"I want you to remember that we walk into our destiny and there is nobody or no devil in hell that can block what God has for you. Bev, go and be a blessing to those young people who for so many years you have dedicated your life, time, and love to."

Beverly with tears in her eyes said to the woman that had made such an impact on her life, "Thank you Pastor, for those words of encouragement, I needed to hear those words coming from you, because you never sugar coat anything you say, so, I believe and receive your blessing in Jesus' name."

Then Pastor D.E. Wright said something Beverly didn't expect. Bev don't think for a minute God doesn't know your heart; you may never leave here. Her next question was about Anita and Amber because she knew they were close.

"Were they staying or going with you?" Pastor asked.

"Well Pastor Beverly answered, to tell the truth, I haven't discussed this with Anita, but I would be lying if I said I didn't pray they are willing to relocate with me. I believe that, after she experienced so much after her husband was killed, she tried so hard to function normally. I know first-hand there were nights she cried herself to sleep. They have moved into my house because she can't stay in hers for too long without having nightmares about that day.

"You remember her telling us about that day when those officers knocked on her door and told her that her husband had been killed."

"Yes, I did, Bev, it was a sad day for everyone. Well, Bev," Pastor said, "I pray that she feels the same way you do and agrees that a move might help her heal and make her realize that she has to let go and let God."

Please ask her to come and see me, especially if she decides to relocate before you leave." "I definitely will do that Beverly said. Pastor thank you and God bless you."

Anita and Amber were at their place packing up whatever was left in their closets since they were about to move out of their place and completely into Beverly's house. Amber packed up all her clothes in a large suitcase because she didn't want to have to return. Anita laughed at her daughter and said "Amber is that all your clothes? Are there anymore here?"

"No Mom, that's it for me." "Well, Amber I guess I'll follow your lead and take all mine over too because, in a day or two, we won't be living here anymore. How do you feel about this move, baby girl?"

"Mom truthfully, since Dad, {Anita's second husband, David} died I didn't want to stay here and what made it worse is that crazy ex-boyfriend of mine might just be stupid enough to pop-up here."

Anita which glanced over at her daughter and replied, "We definitely don't want that to happen, you father would kill him for sure." "Reggie would most likely get close to killing him and that's for sure."

"I love being at Auntie Bev's house. We've always felt like family besides we're there more than here, anyway mom. I think dad would like that we're staying with Auntie. This place has too many sad memories. You don't have those nightmares over there either, mom."

Anita said, "that's true and I feel great being around her also. So, we're both alright with this move, Amber, it may not be a permanent move but while it lasts let's enjoy! Agreed?" "Yes, I agree Mom."

Amber sat on the floor with tears in her eyes recalling spending holidays with her dad. He always took her to pick out the Christmas tree, and they always bought the tallest home. They would buy the decorations together and then decorate the tree on Christmas Eve and not a day sooner. By the time Anita woke up on Christmas morning the tree was beautifully decorated, and they wrapped all the presents, they both remember those times with David.

Tears fell uncontrollably now because she missed her stepdad so much, but she felt that he was her angel watching over her, pushing her in the right directions of life. She smiled through her tears when she thought about all the good times they had together. He will always be in their hearts.

Her first bike ride, first camping experience, swimming lessons, birthdays, those nightly bedtime stories just before she dozed off to sleep.

How he just loved Anita, it was almost like a fairytale she was his Queen, and he was her King. He always told Amber she was the prettiest girl in town and would always be his princess.

Amber and Anita cherished the time they spent together because he was always leaving for another assignment with the service that would take him away from them for months, sometimes years at a time.

Amber, said, "Mom I only have you and Auntie and my grandparents," and after that incident with Jerome she wouldn't let them down again.

David was her encourager, and she remembered everything he taught her about becoming a young lady and wouldn't accept anything less from her. She knew even though he had passed on she still felt that she couldn't let him down. So even though they would be moving to another house or even another state where she wouldn't know anyone, she promised to do her best to honor both her dad's.

Back at Beverly's house Anita began preparing dinner, and Beverly started telling them about the promotion that she had accepted. Everything was fine, Anita and Amber were excited for Beverly until she mentioned that this position meant that she would have to relocate to another state.

Amber said, "What! Another state Auntie? Oh NO!" Anita was sitting at the table cutting the vegetables up, she didn't say anything because she didn't really know what to say or think yet.

"Wait, Amber let me finish, it's not really far. At first, the company wanted to open another office in Arizona, but they finally decided Washington needed the services more."

"There are a few ways this could work in our favor, Amber, you could transfer your credits to a college out there, or you can commute.

Anita, you could open your business out here or there, we would have to really see how that would work out also."

"The company is giving me a house, a car and pay increase. I didn't want to leave you here if you wanted to go, but that's up to you Sis. I was also thinking about me staying out there weekly and returning here on weekends.

I'm not sure if that's feasible, but we could try it out and see. Since Johnathan is going into this venture with me, I could possibly work from here a few days a week."

"I'd have to discuss this with our C.E.O. and the board members here first. Somewhere in the back of her mind she was still not one-hundred percent sure. Second thought were creeping in her mind. *Do I really want to give up my house here or my church family?*

So, I still have a lot to think through and discuss with my partner Johnathan who is also feeling unsure because of his mom's health issues."

"I know it's a lot to digest, but I want everyone to be happy and content with my decision. I believe my Father in Heaven will work it out for us. I'm sure of it without a doubt, Sis, you're not saying much over there, Why?"

Anita looked at Bev and said, "I just don't know what to say Sis, but like you just said, our Father will work it out for us. So, if that's His will for us, then I'll follow and obey His will and not complain."

"God has been too good to me for me to question His plans now Sis. If it's a change we need to do, then so be it." They all joined in a big hug and said "Amen."

Anita said, "I have learned that we may not understand the whys and why nots, but through our faith in Jesus, I'm sure that He wouldn't forsake us, and if we follow His will for our lives, we will be happy and at peace.

Better than if we try doing things our way and trying to make decisions without praying for guidance from the Lord."

"So again, if it's done through faith and prayer, I'm

good, right Amber?" Anita looking at her daughter smiling, Amber shook her head in agreement. "Mom, Auntie I might not like it, but you both are right. I believe in the Lord with all my heart." "Ok then, let's eat because it smells good up in here ladies."

Everyone sat down to enjoy a well-seasoned, and tasty meal, prepared by Anita. After cleaning up the kitchen, they decided to meet back in an hour and enjoy a movie in the theater room downstairs. They weren't going to talk about this move until it needed to be discussed again, and it would have to be, but not tonight.

Beverly went upstairs and called Johnathan, once he answered she told him about the talk she had with Anita and Amber and they agreed with the idea that they might need to relocate.

Beverly said, "John, how's your mother? We've known each other for a long time and you never really spoke of your mom or your sister."

Johnathan response was, "Bev you're right but I never wanted to really mix my family problems with the company business."

"John, you should know me better than that. We're friends, and you should never feel that you can't share your family issues with me." Johnathan got quiet for a few minutes, then he said, "Bev you're right I'm sorry. I didn't want people feeling sorry for me. We've been able to handle the family issues for all this time."

Beverly interrupted him, "Johnathan, what are you doing now? Would you like to come over and watch a movie with us? I want to hear what's going on if you feel like talking about it. I'm not pressuring you. You can't keep all this to yourself, it's not healthy, we are friends. Don't you ever forget that?"

"Bev, I don't want to burden you." Johnathan said. "It is never a burden when a friend is going through something. Please come over," Johnathan replied, "ok, alright, Bev, give me a few minutes I'll be over. And thank you." "You're welcome Johnathan."

Once Johnathan arrived about a half an hour later, they invited him to come and enjoy the movie and offered him some food. He told them he had eaten, but he would enjoy the movie and a glass of wine with them. After the movie, Beverly, Anita, and Johnathan spoke regarding what he had just encountered with his sister and mother.

Beverly felt heartbroken for him but relieved that his mother had been found and was being cared for properly at the nursing home.

Anita opened a bottle of fine red wine for them, and they sat and drank and talked into the late evening. Johnathan promised Beverly and Anita that he would not ever again keep anything in regard to his family from them. "It's getting late. Thanks for the movie and the company and most of all for allowing me to vent my feelings to both for you."

Beverly said, "John anything that we can do to help you or your sister in any capacity let us know, promise?"

Johnathan said, "Yes I will and thanks again, I should be leaving now ladies, see you Sunday."

Anita and Beverly waving, "Good night John get home safe. Oh, I'd like to see your twin sister." Beverly added; "I really don't remember her. It's been a while since I last saw her, maybe a few years, ago right?" I'll make it happen, thanks again, ladies," as Johnathan left.

"Wow, Sis, it's true we might think our problems are bad, but there's always somebody else's doing worse. Anita, it's hard to believe that Johnathan wouldn't feel that he could have talked to us about his family issues. We have always included him in most of our personal problems; well not all, but some."

Beverly said, "you know men are different from us woman. We vent our feelings to one another; men don't do that." "Well, I'm happy that he feels that he can openly talk with us about it now without criticism or shame, replied Anita. Then Anita said, "I'll take another glass of wine how about you Sis?" "I'll second that Sis."

While enjoying their wine, Anita began telling Bev how Amber was talking about her dad, David and how she missed him. "Then she asked me about your dad and why you never talk about your parents or your childhood." Beverly sipped her wine listening intently to this conversation. "Oh! what did you tell her Sis?"

"I said, some people don't want to remember their past let alone talk about it. She wants to know about your past, and how you got to this point in your life." "Well Nita, I have ten journals addressing that subject, that I haven't opened in years. I never thought anyone would be interested in knowing my past. Certainly not a young girl."

"You know we discussed it years ago when we first met and began talking about our childhoods. I'm not sure I want to even discuss those days. But when I think about my journals maybe just maybe she could learn from some of the experiences I went through. They might help Amber understand my drive for success."

"My childhood wasn't something I wanted to share, but again maybe now that I'm at this point in my life sharing could be a good thing. What do you think about that Nita?"

Anita said, "Sis, that is your call, but I think she understands that although we may not start out with a good childhood doesn't mean we have to end up with a bad life. It's up to us to want to fill those **VOIDS** with a *Victory Over Instant Disappointments.* **VOIDS,** are something many of us have in our lives."

Beverly and Anita finished their drinks and straightened up the theater room and talked about some things to move upstairs. Bev asked Anita, "Is the furniture that's upstairs enough for the rooms, or was there anything you need?" Anita assured Bev that the upstairs was starting to look great and of course Amber wanted to paint her room some odd color.

"Nita it's her space, and she can paint it any way she wants." "See there you go again, Bev, spoiling her." They laughed so hard their eyes were tearing up. After finishing the bottle of wine, Bev was headed upstairs. Anita wanted to prepare some hors-d'oeuvres dips to drop off tomorrow for a client.

"Oh Sis, by the way, how is your business going? I've been so consumed with the new position and Johnathan until we haven't made time to discuss your business, Sorry, about that."

Anita said, "wait a minute don't you dare apologize for anything, we've both been busy, and I wasn't feeling left out because we always catch up sooner or later, we do live in the same house. But since you're asking, my business is doing well and my clientele has grown to forty-five."

"Forty-five wow! That's a blessing, Sis." "Yes, it is Bev" Beverly was walking toward the steps, "Good night Sis." Anita said, "Oh yeah, I also haven't had time to tell you about this guy I've met, one of my client's brothers." "Wait, what Nita, are you kidding me a man really? Oh, darling, we must talk!"

"What's his name? what does he look like? how old is he?" "Hey, slow down Sis, his name is Malcolm, and yes he's good looking. You know the kind I like, and he's in his late 40's but we haven't been on a date yet;" "That's a good start Nita, loving it." Beverly was smiling at her friend.

Anita reminded Beverly, "You need a date night. You are always working. Don't become a work-a-holic like Johnathan or you know who, pointing to herself, please."

Beverly sat on her chaise in her bedroom thinking about Amber and the questions she might be asking her about her youth. Beverly sat there almost visualizing word for word in those journals that were under her bed and had been there since she moved into this house years ago. She was hoping never to open that trunk again not wanting to do anything but dismiss the hurtful memories. She didn't want to ever remember them.

She struggled for years to forgive and forget her past. The strongholds that had her blaming herself for every disappointment, that made it hard to believe that she should be successful. She no longer blamed herself for the disappointments that filtered into her adulthood.

The disappointments, obstacles and setbacks have turned into victories. God allowed her to go through the **VOID'S** so she could help another young woman, a friend, or a family member succeed in their life.

She could witness to them on how she came through it all. She is now stronger and wiser than she would have ever been if she let the enemy win. So as far as Bev was concerned that trunk was staying exactly where it was, and she had no intentions of opening it.

But, Amber, what was she going to tell her? What questions might she be asking? How deep would she be going into her past? Beverly said to herself, *"Bev, you know you're going to lose this one, right?"*

Beverly loved Amber, and she felt that her past could possibly help her to not make some of the mistakes most young women make. The wrong choices in men, thinking to work minimum wage jobs is better than getting a higher education and not putting God first in their lives.

Amber has a good head on her shoulders, and she is completing her education. The encounter with Jerome had given her a different outlook on young men, especially the ones that didn't respect young women. Anita and Reggie had educated their daughter when and how to save her money. Was there much else left for her learn? Yes, life in general.

Beverly knew there would be always something to learn in life and unlike herself, Amber had two experienced women that hopefully will continue to teach her how to prevent the pitfalls of life.

So many young girls' lives might have turned out different if they had someone to help them make positive decisions. There were always young girls and young men that wouldn't listen until it's too late wanting to find their own way themselves.

As young women, we go through the stigma of being a woman and being a black woman. To become successful, we must be on top of our game, work harder, think smarter, learn and make sacrifices.

We need a strong foundation which is the church because if we stray, we'll return to our roots. Our foundation is the Word of God.

Beverly would have a nice talk about her younger days and see what Amber really wanted to know and then she would decide if she should open those books or not. Until then she'll be writing in the journal that is by her bedside, and it usually reveals a happier time in her life. Her victory is that she had overcome all those disappointments from her past.

Well, for now, Bev didn't really know how she would handle this situation until it occurred, so for tonight, she was going to sleep because she was overthinking as usual.

The next weeks would be hectic due to Johnathan and Beverly having to return to Washington to determine approximately how long it will take to complete both projects.

There were several conference calls between the managers and the executives along with the contractors.

They couldn't secure a building large enough to accommodate all the equipment, staff, and other necessary offices yet. Also, Arizona was not sure that this venture would benefit the needs of the unemployed.

This was a strange conversation for a state that had a 75% unemployment rate. So, Johnathan was arranging a meeting with the Mayor and the planning board to fully explain the benefits of this amazing project and the opportunity for job growth.

They would be flying out to Washington, to visit a few sites to secure a building large enough to accommodate this company plan.

Johnathan didn't feel that this should be completed until the final reports came back and were discussed so there may be a change in plans regarding the visit. Erika and Beverly had been in constant contact discussing the incidents that occurred.

They were concerned that the problems may affect developments and the Board would question if these plans would be agreed upon in a reasonable timeframe. Erika was feeling stressed because the plans seemed to be unraveling right before her eyes.

Erika's husband had expressed some concern about her always looking weak and tired. He spoke to her about it, but she totally ignored it by saying, "It's just I have a lot on my plate right now, with the new projects and some problems that have arisen. I'm fine honey, no need for concern, love you."

Beverly decided that before she left for these meetings, she wanted a girls' night out. She got a call from an old girlfriend, Pamela who she hadn't heard from since last year. They talked for a while, and they caught up on old times. They talked about how their lives were evolving.

Pamela knew Anita and her daughter also, so they agreed that a girls' night out was a wonderful idea.

"How about a movie and dinner after?" Pamela suggested. Beverly responded, "Before I fully agree let me check with Anita so she can check her schedule. I doubt if Amber wants to hang out with us old ladies." They laughed at that statement.

Pamela said, "Alright, just let me know, I'll be in your part of town for two weeks and would love to see you guys."

Beverly replied was, "that sounds good to me, I'll get back to you in a day or two. Good talking to you girlfriend tell your mom I said hello." At that point, they hung up.

Later that evening Bev said to Anita. "Sis, guess who called me after all this time?" Anita said, "Why do you do that? You know I never guess correctly. Who is it, Bev?" "Pamela! remember her?" Anita thought for a moment then said, "OH! yes, I do how is she these days?" "Didn't she move to Brooklyn for that new job offer?"

Beverly looked shocked for just a second. "That's right Sis I totally forgot about that, she's visiting her mom and wants to catch up with us before she leaves town again."

"I suggested a girls' night out; do you have any free time busy lady?" "I can always make time for a girls' night out we definitely need one. When is this date happening? Soon I hope."

At that moment Amber came in, and she had overheard some of the conversation. "What's up Mom?" "Oh, hi baby girl" Anita answered, "Mom! Auntie can you please ask Mom to stop calling me that. I'm not a baby or a girl well I am a girl," she laughed. Anita and Bev both looked at each other like is she serious?

"Baby girl will continue to be your name lady, even if you're a married lady understood?" her mom said.

Amber put on her little girl face and just walked away. "Oh, wait baby girl" Amber slowly turned around. "Yes Auntie?" "Would you like to hang out with old ladies Friday for a movie and dinner?"

Amber shrugged her shoulders and laughed saying, "Sorry but I planned to hang out with some Generation X girls this weekend. I know you know who the Generation X girls are right?"

She walked away laughing. As she was walking away Beverly, teasing saying, "Oh those groupies, right? As she left the room."

"I'm hoping for Friday because I also have a hectic schedule. I'll contact Pamela and let's see if it works for everyone. Meanwhile, how's the business going Anita? Seems you've been really busy."

"Bev, you won't believe it, but my business has grown through word of mouth. I haven't even had time to advertise, but I keep getting orders and generally large ones from corporations."

"It's either birthday parties, retirement parties, baby showers, or holidays parties. It's been crazy, but I'm just so blessed and thankful to God for this breakthrough. I have to bring in a few of the students from the culinary school to assist me that's how busy I've been.

It's exciting, and I'm grateful for Amber too she comes to help whenever she has time. She's keeping busy, and I'm glad for that."

Then Beverly called Pamela leaving a message letting her know that if Friday was good for her, then they can meet up. Pamela was the woman that always seemed to get into messy situations with no sensible reason why. Pamela called Beverly back after a few minutes and told her she had theater tickets to see, "Mama I Want to Sing". Beverly said okay that sounds great.

So, although Beverly was meeting up with her, she wasn't too sure just how much of her business she would be sharing with Pamela. Anita was the one who reminded her of the last time they were together.

Though it was about a year ago, it turned out to be a complete disaster. Pamela trying to take some guy home and his girlfriend was ready to fight Pamela over her boyfriend.

Pamela was too old to be fighting anyone especially a girl half her age.

Hopefully, she matured some, or matured a lot since then. When Friday rolled around the girls met up in front of the theater and Pamela handed them their tickets to see "Mama I Want to Sing" by Vy Higginsen

Entering the theater their seats were close to the stage and just before the play began a couple came in and sat directly in front of them. Pamela smiled at the handsome man, and he gestured with a return smile. Pamela whispered to Beverly, "He's cute and sexy right Bev?"

Beverly looked at her in bewilderment, not sure how to answer that question. Beverly noticed that he was with his wife because they both had on matching wedding rings.

The strange thing was that throughout the entire play Pamela would lean forward and touch the man's shoulder almost like caressing it. Beverly nudged Anita making her aware of what was going on. They couldn't believe their eyes.

Anita went as far as clearing her throat several times hoping to send a silent message to Pamela, however, that didn't help. This was making both Anita and Beverly uncomfortable, but they tried to concentrate on the play, which was excellent. Beverly couldn't wait for intermission to confront Pamela.

After stepping into the lobby, Anita grabbed Pamela and said, "What in the hell were you thinking? Please tell us why you were touching that man?" Beverly interjected, "What's wrong with you girl?" Beverly and Anita were whispering so as not to draw attention to themselves. Pamela looked slyly at them and blatantly said, "He's my man, not hers.

That will be over soon; he promised me it would." And we just happened to have seats right behind him how did that happen Pam? "Please explain this," Anita demanded.

Pamela went on explaining that she had tickets that he gave her, "HER MAN" as she called him. "Oh, so we just happened to be invited with tickets you already had other plans for, Pam?" Anita sighed. Pamela sarcastically said, "Well it worked out we're all here, right?" Beverly looked at Anita and just sighed.

While they were standing there talking the same man walked near them and tapped Pamela on her behind. The woman he was with had gone to the ladies' room.

Pamela stood directly in front of him, and he looked her up and down with lust in his eyes; Anita pulled Pamela away as fast as she could.

They all returned to their seats for the second half of this amazing play.

Pamela continued flirting with this man through the second half of the play until Beverly pinched Pamela so hard, she said "OUCH!"

As they were exiting the building, Pamela was searching for "HER MAN" once she saw him, she waved, but he didn't wave back. He acted like he didn't notice her waving in his direction. Anita noticed him also looking in their direction she turned her back to him and said. "it won't go on much longer" and walked away; Anita didn't even look back to see his expression. "Let's go, girlfriend, we need a cool drink." They headed for the restaurant. Beverly agreed, "Yes because I need to make some sense of all that just happened."

As they began walking Pamela waved at him not aware that his wife was directly behind them and apparently realized that Pam was waving at her husband. The woman caught up to them and stepped in front of Pamela. Beverly and Anita were observing a street entertainer, so they never noticed the exchange, and now it was too late. Pamela began walking toward her friends.

The woman moved awfully close to the ladies and introduced herself as Mrs. Robert Milner. She politely asked Anita if she was the caterer that had catered Police Captain Farrell's retirement party? Pamela was so shocked she couldn't speak at first, caught off guard.

Anita replied, "Yes I did, were you there?" Mrs. Milner smiled and said "Yes" I'm a detective out of that precinct. The food was so good that day I'm sure we all ate too much.

The woman went on to say that she works long hours as a police detective and when she and her husband can catch up and have a date night, they love spending time together.

We started to end the conversation when Mrs. Milner looked directly at Pamela and smiled and said, "Marriage is a covenant, and no man or woman will separate them." Pamela couldn't look directly at the woman.

She tried to hide her pain and hurt so she quickly excused herself and told Mrs. Milner, it was nice meeting her.

After that encounter, Pamela hopefully would come to her senses and realize that that man is not leaving his wife anytime soon and she's a woman with a legal gun. Beverly thought to herself, *Girl this is crazy.*

After they were seated in the restaurant, Pamela was sad and told her girlfriends she was embarrassed. She went on to say "I ruined the evening, didn't I? I'm always ruining something marriage, dates, you name it. I'm always destroying everything I get involved with." Anita was heated by this time stating, "stop the crap we are not interested in your pity party. You're wrong, and you need to admit it to yourself and God."

Pamela looked at them strangely, "what are you saying? God doesn't know me. I'm always doing something politically incorrect, okay." Anita said, "Okay? Wait, how long have you been seeing this man? Didn't you know he was married? and married to a police detective?

She's always in the newspaper, she does take her job very seriously. We'll get to God in a minute, but you need to own up to what you've done and be real about the damage it has caused you, Pam."

"Don't hate on a sister, he didn't let me know he was married until a few months ago." Beverly said, "What, a few months ago, really Pam?" "Look!" Pam said, "I need a man to complete me, and he fit the description exactly." Beverly went on to say, "wait, we don't need a man to complete us, we need Jesus, the Alpha and Omega of our lives.

Number two he's an adulterer and a liar. Oh, what exactly was he doing for you, Pam?" "He loved me at least that's what he told me."

"You believed him, right?" "Yes, Bev, I did, "Look at him wouldn't you have, believed him?" Anita was upset by this time and said, "NO! girl, the first reason is that he's married."

Pam continued, "We'd meet almost every day at lunchtime, and some evenings we took long drives and stayed at a bed and breakfast on many weekends."

"I felt secure around him, okay, I loved him, well I still do, but I guess that's over now that he allowed his wife to come in my face like that."

Beverly said, "Listen to yourself, accusing everyone but yourself. You chose to have an adulterous relationship that's going nowhere. He's not leaving his wife obviously you realize that Pam?" "NO!" Pam said," "He buys me expensive jewelry and diamond rings. He even pays my rent sometimes." Beverly tapped Pam on her shoulder listen, "Pamela, you've got a decent job right, and what are you doing that you can't buy yourself nice things?" Pamela continued "If I could, I wouldn't need a man don't you understand?

Anita voice went up an octave, "No we don't Pam. Listen don't you think you deserve a man that loves you for who you are? That's like hush money the material things don't signify true love. This guy is using you; he doesn't love you. When a man loves a woman, there nothing he won't do for her, and they are together through bad and good times," not only when he can slip away, or his wife is working late. Girl, you're wasting good years on a lost cause. Wait on God, and he'll bring you the man that he created just for you trust me when I say this and work on you."

Then Pam said, "Wait a minute, the last time I checked neither one of you had a man, so how can you tell me to wait on one? That's what you both are doing. Waiting?" Anita continued explaining, "Hold up Pam, seriously I had one of the greatest husbands a woman could ask for, but unfortunately he died in combat. When we were together, I knew that he loved me with every fiber of his being and vice-versa. We shared everything together good times and bad. Although when I think about it, there weren't too many bad times." "Beverly, what's your excuse?" asked Pam.

"Well, to tell the truth, my marriage had its ups and downs, but we all learn from every experience, that I can tell you."

Pamela sat there with tears in her eyes saying, "Bev, Nita I know you're probably right, but I hate being alone and lonely, I want love just like anyone else and I believed him. What am I supposed to do be lonely and sad, or live my life the way I want to?"

Beverly went on to say, "Pam, we understand, and before I accepted God into my life again, I probably felt a lot like you, but I need you to hear us clearly. There is no greater Love than God's unconditional love. He loves us even in our mess and life is too precious and short to waste it on someone who's married. Unless he's married to you, girlfriend. You're a smart, beautiful, intelligent woman, and there is a man that wants you for who you are. But first, you must love yourself, first learn to love you."

"Honey" Anita interjected, "find a God Word-based church and learn to love Jesus because He will help heal your pain and hurt that you're holding from your past. I know how that feels, and now I am free and at peace with all my past hurts. So, Pam, you have to make a choice to seek the Lord and allow Him to heal you and prepare you to be a wife."

"The Lord is a forgiving God when we accept Him in our lives. At this moment you may not want to hear about how good God is, but sooner or later hopefully sooner, you'll realize that without Jesus in your life we're nothing but sinners living sinful lives." Anita said "we're not here to condemn, we love you Pam."

Anita saw the waiter coming with their food and said, "Let's eat and give Pam some time to digest this conversation. Hopefully, this little counseling session will put some things in perspective. Please understand Pam we love you and want the best for you girl."

Pamela sat there not saying anything throughout the meal. When they finished, she thanked them for meeting her and hoped they got home safely.

They headed for their cars hugged each other and left. Once Pamela got in her car, she started driving off then had to pull over because she started sobbing uncontrollably, she knew she needed to make some changes in her meaningless life. She wasn't sure how to start or where to begin. Maybe she would talk to Beverly in a few days, she knew Beverly and Anita cared.

On their way home Anita said, "Sis did you know this beforehand, she had always been reckless. I truly hope our counseling session helped her think about her actions and changing her lifestyle."

Bev said, "I wish I had, but unfortunately I didn't, but like you said we both hope we made an impact on her to want to change her life and seek Jesus. I pray she ends that so-called love affair with that guy. The truth is many women feel the same way she does, they would rather have any man in their life rather than wait for a godly man."

"Sis," Beverly said to Anita," "Do you think God has a man for us again, I mean don't you think about it sometimes?" "Well to tell the truth I really haven't had time to sit down and think about a man.

My life doesn't allow me to fit a man into my hectic lifestyle now. You know my business, my daughter, my clients, but I told you I met a nice guy and we talk every day."

"I think I would like a husband again someday." "Wait a minute Bev you've been dodging Johnathan for years, when are you going to let him in your life? Sis don't wait too long."

"Oh, really, me and Johnathan, I don't think that's going to work we work together, and he's a good friend, and that's what makes it difficult." They laughed and said, "We'll wait, that's what we're going to agree on. Yes, Sis, I agree.""

"But really Beverly you know you're feeling Johnathan and I know it too. And friends make wonderful husbands. Remember David was my dedicated best friend first before he was my loving, caring husband."

Beverly didn't respond because she did like Johnathan, but she wasn't sure how he felt or even if he was somewhat interested in her like that. For now, business partners worked for her.

Then Anita asked a difficult question, "Beverly, are you really going to relocate? That's a hard pill to swallow isn't its Sis? You can be honest about this it's me you're talking to!" Bev. "Anita this is the hardest pill I've had to swallow. The opportunity is a great one and you know I love helping our youth, but giving up my place, our place and what about your business? Have you thought about what you're going to do with that? You're not in the position to up and leave when it's going so well right now." I don't think I could ask you to do that, I'm not that selfish. I've accepted the position but deep down inside the move, I'm not feeling it, Sis. I'm not too sure that Johnathan is feeling it either, not with his mother's condition getting worse."

"Anita, I've prayed on this and really didn't get a clear answer except that the Holy Spirit told me "Be prepared for change."

Anita responded, "Well that just means Beverly Jensen that we must let the Lord work it out and our faith is strong enough, deep enough that whatever the outcome we will have the victory." "Amen," replied Beverly.

"Anita in a few days Johnathan and I will be flying to Washington, to sit down with the contractors to go over the building plans. The contractors have questions and concerns about this project and who would be directing the planning. The Board of Directors is dealing with the situation from what I understand something they don't usually get involved in."

"Johnathan is good at handling that part isn't he Sis?" "Yes, he is, I believe that's one of the reasons they chose him to work with me on these projects. He's been to several other states and countries to discuss this new venture and offer other countries the opportunity to collaborate with our company. I know he's done well with those developments."

Then, Anita said, Our Indian summer is just about over, have you felt the mornings?" Don't remind me Beverly said, "They have been quite chilly, I'll make sure I pack for the weather."

The days went by fast, and before Beverly realized, it was time to leave for again. Johnathan was there on time as usual. Again, Anita was up and had some homemade cranberry muffins and hot coffee waiting for them.

Johnathan said, "Nita you're cooking is the best." Beverly walked into the kitchen and said, "Yes, but Sis you didn't have to get up at this dreadful hour, it's 4:30 a.m." "It's alright, let's pray for a safe trip and that everything works out in perfect order."

They held hands and Anita begun praying then said, "Love you both."

They walked to the rental car on route to the airport. While driving, one of Beverly's favorite song was playing on the radio, "For Every Mountain" by the Brooklyn Tabernacle Choir.

Every time she hears this song it brings tears to her eyes, that song touches her heart in ways only Christ above knows.

Bev remembers playing this song for almost twenty-four hours and many days that song helped her make it through her pain.

There is always a song or Scripture that touches us in a very spiritual way. This song did. Then she noticed that Johnathan was singing the song too. She thought to herself, *Well, alright let's praise the LORD before getting on this plane.*

They were getting their praise on in the car. Once at the airport and checking the schedule again to make sure the flight was on time, they went to the section where Delta would be loading. Not long after that they entered the plane and took their seats in first class.

The attendant offered them coffee or tea, but they declined, they just wanted to catch up on some sleep.

They weren't used to getting up this early. Beverly thanked Johnathan because with all his traveling, this hour wasn't early to him at all.

By the time the flight started, it would be close to eight anyway. Hours had passed so far; the trip was comfortable.

Beverly went into a deep sleep and was dreaming about her dad and how she seemed to be running around looking for him, but every time she saw him, he'd disappear again.

The plane had hit some turbulence, and that's what woke Bev up, she gripped the handles of her seat. Johnathan placed his hand over hers to try and comfort her, he realized that she had been sleeping and whatever she had dreamt didn't sit well with her spirit. There was a second dip and the passengers begun to realize that the plane was in severe turbulence.

The flight attendant was on the loudspeaker system telling all the passengers to make sure their seatbelts were on and to listen for further instructions. Beverly was starting to get a little nervous, but somewhere deep down in her spirit she knew God was in charge. Then the pilot was on the loudspeaker telling the passengers to stay calm we should pass through the storm momentarily.

All we heard was sighs of relief throughout the plane. Beverly glanced over at Johnathan who also had a serious look on his face. He wasn't really that concerned because he'd experienced this occurrence many times before.

Johnathan didn't say much, just assured her, "We'll be fine Bev." Then she glanced out the window but couldn't see anything but a storm and dark clouds.

Meanwhile back in New York Mrs. Brownstone had been on the phone all morning talking with contractors that had reported a glitch in the plans, that could possibly put a hold on this project. There was a water line bust that wiped out much of the area they were planning to build on. This was a problem that the city officials had known about for years and did nothing to fix.

Erika insistently explained to the contractors that her people were on their way to Washington.

You remember Mr. Sheppard and Ms. Jensen don't you Stephen? "Yes, Ms. Brownstone I have spoken with them several times."

Stephen and Jesse Zuckerman were the contractors on this project, and they weren't too happy with the latest developments. Stephen said, I expect a full report from my people on this mess.

Now, this might hold up everything for a week or maybe months. This concerned Erika, in fact, she was overly concerned about this latest information.

Erika sighed deeply and thought, *"This is a disaster."* She had to tell the Board, Johnathan, and Beverly as soon as possible.

The plane took another dive that caused screams from the passengers. And suddenly she found herself praying and thinking *"Lord if this is it, please forgive all my sins, I repent from the depths of my heart."*

Glancing out the window Beverly thoughts went back in time. *Beverly the little girl and her dad telling her in the funeral car that she would not be staying with him anymore and she couldn't understand why he'd pick that particular day and time to tell her this life-changing decision.*

Beverly loved her dad even though he abandoned her early in her life.

Beverly as a child thought she and her daddy would always be together like most little girls. Now at this moment, she was grateful that the Lord taught her to forgive and to love herself. To learn who God was for her life and put her trust in Him. Johnathan was saying "Bev, Bev you okay?"

Johnathan looked at Beverly, and they both said, "It feels like the plane was circling around or we're turning around." After a few minutes, the flight attendant announced that due to a heavy rainstorm in Delaware and turbulent weather conditions in a few other states, they were instructed to make a landing at the nearest airport, the plane was going to return to Chicago airport and land before the weather got any worse.

"Hopefully, we'll make it there safely." Beverly overheard a woman behind them say. She turned around and said, "Pray." Erika had made several attempts to contact them to no avail.

The weather conditions had made pager contact almost impossible. People were getting frustrated because they could not notify family members to give them updates.

This meant that they would have to wait until the plane landed if it ever did. Johnathan began to silently pray for a safe landing.

In the back of the plane, women yelled, "We better start praying like our lives depended on it up in here."

By then some passengers agreed, and if you listened closely you might even hear some praying quietly. The flight attendants were working to try and keep the passengers calm. Johnathan and Beverly said, "thank you, Jesus."

This reminded Johnathan of the story about how they walked around the wall of Jericho. It was amazing. People know there is power in the Name of Jesus, and they needed His power at this very moment. People got happy and almost forgot where they were and what was happening until a deep dip stopped everything instantly.

Another announcement came over the loudspeaker, "Please turn off all electronics immediately and make sure all seat belts are fastened." Silence came over the entire plane at that second. Passengers went back into their own thoughts.

Anita had overheard the weather report on her drive home, and when she got in the house, she also attempted to contact Beverly and Johnathan but could not get any response. Anita was calling Carol to see if she had heard anything from either one of them by now.

Carol told Anita that she was concerned about the weather also but knowing those two they prayed up the entire plane and would be fine, not to worry. "So, let's not worry because girl you know prayers and worry don't fit in the same box."

Anita smiled and said, "Carol you are so right." I'll feel a lot better when we hear from one of them, though, you know what I mean?"

"Girl, but there's supposed to be a tornado brewing in that area." At that very moment, they began to pray for safe travel for not only Bev and John but everyone that was traveling today.

It was not until the next evening around 7:30 p.m. that Anita hears the house phone ring.

She answered it hoping it was Beverly or Johnathan. "Hello, Bev, John," before the person on the other end could answer, "Nita it's Johnathan," Thank God!" Anita said, "I was beginning to get a little concerned because we hadn't heard from either of you." Johnathan said, "Thank God we were able to land safely."

"I know it was a little crazy. We had to turn around and reroute to Chicago because the weather is horrible in Delaware.

We're in Chicago due to the weather conditions. It was a little scary for a while, but everyone is safe. There were some passengers that started praying. I had never encountered anything like that before, it was powerful, Nita."

"John, Bev, where is she?" Anita asked. "Oh, she is ordering us some food from across the street, and we'll be staying in the hotel up the block until we get a rescheduled flight. Wait I see her coming, hold on Nita."

Beverly walked up to Johnathan and handed him the bags and asked "Is that Anita? "Yes," and he handed her the phone. "Sorry Sis, we had no reception to contact you until we landed here in Chi-town.

The storm is bad, and most of the flights have been canceled, so we don't know how long we'll here. We're safe, and we've got two rooms in the hotel. How is Amber and everything at home?"

Anita didn't want to tell her be how worried she really was until she called Carol. "Amber is great, she went to a basketball game, she'll be home later.

I'll tell her to call you if it's not too late. Is that okay Sis?" "Yes," Beverly said, "Of course, call me anytime. I miss you both, you know this trip is important, and it seems the enemy is trying to make it difficult, but we know "God is in charge." Just then Anita remembered,

"Erika has been trying to contact you or John, her message stated she needed to speak to one of you as soon as possible. Beverly thought to herself, OH LORD", *what now?*

"Anita okay let me call her and find out what's happening on that end. I'll get back to you later, Love you, Sis." Anita replied, "same here," and they hung up.

Johnathan stood up and said, "Bev can we go to the hotel now, so we can eat?" "Oh, John yes I'm sorry. Let's go, I'm bushed," "Me too." They left the airport, hailed a taxi, and headed for the hotel; it wasn't easy finding rooms because most of the passengers were booking rooms also.

The hotel was expensive, but Beverly had the company's credit card but to her surprise she didn't even have to use because the company had already paid for everything.

Once checked in, Johnathan realized that they had adjoining suites. Beverly was impressed, the company had arranged for them to have suites instead of rooms and all the amenities were covered too.

Erika had contacted the airlines when she couldn't contact her people and made the provisions for them. After being told the conditions, the airplane was facing she called and made the arrangements for them to have the best for their entire stay.

Johnathan asked, "Bev, is it alright to eat dinner with you and then crash in my suite and let you get some rest too?" "John I'm exhausted, so maybe it would be better if we just eat in our own suites."

I need a shower, and I'm so ready to lay down. Johnathan was hoping for a different answer, but he knew she was tired, so he said, "I fully understand Bev, Good night, get some rest." "Good night John."

Oh Bev, "I'll contact Erika tomorrow and find out exactly what is going on." "Thanks, John."

As Johnathan was leaving Beverly called him back and said, "Come in let's eat." He smiled to himself and set his food on the table and ordered some hot tea for them both. This was a nice beginning to what might be a long haul together.

After some interesting conversation and good food, Johnathan said his, "Good night again Bev." When Johnathan entered his room, there was a message left on the answering machine making Johnathan aware that they would be notified when another flight was leaving for Washington and that all charges were paid for through their company and to please enjoy the stay, compliments of the hotel.

After a relaxing bath in the fabulous jet stream tub, Beverly climbed into the bed when the phone rang. She couldn't make herself answer that phone call, hoping they would leave a message allowing her to respond tomorrow morning or whenever she arose.

While lying in bed, Beverly thought, *"I should order some desert."* At that very moment, a light tap was at the door. When she looked, all she could see was a piece of carrot cake. She laughed and opened the door, "you know me too well. I do love dessert before turning in," they both laughed.

Again, they sat down and enjoyed that carrot cake then Johnathan said, "Okay, I'm not going to knock on your door anymore tonight, I promise Bev." "John, you knew I couldn't resist a sweet temptation. Beverly took a fork full and said, "Oh, my goodness this is delicious really John it is."

He said, "I know, I already ate some of mine." Johnathan stood up and walked toward the door again saying, "If we're still here tomorrow, we should try the diner downstairs Bev." "That sounds like a great idea, so we're on for tomorrow John, Good night" and she closed the door.

Sticking her head out she said, "John doesn't the company usually pay for everything? His answer shocked her. He said, "Not everything, the food is always something you are responsible for I've always paid for food myself.

No matter where I traveled, they paid for the hotels and transportation, but not food." "Oh, Beverly said, "That's not too bad, right?" He agreed it was alright with him. Johnathan leaned in and kissed her on the cheek and left her suite.

Beverly walked over to the balcony admiring the beautiful skylight. The city was lit up and reminded her of New York City at night. Then her thoughts went to Johnathan, *wondering how many more times she would see him looking sexy in those silk pajamas.* She smiled to herself and went to bed.

Beverly continued to have recurring dreams for the past month or so. She's a little girl living in the last place she and her dad had stayed before her whole world crumbled around her. She was sitting in the large window seat in her room watching the snow fall, the flakes were always large and so pretty.

In the middle of the night, Beverly awoke to feel a little sad about all that was in her past, but now she was a successful woman. Beverly was grateful for where God had brought her from, she was thankful for His grace and mercy in her life and that He thought it not robbery to love her unconditionally even with her faults.

Every time she thought about how blessed she was it brought tears to her eyes. She felt like a nobody not knowing who she was until she found Jesus.

The Bible grounded her faith in His Word, she knew who she was, and whose she was, A child of The Most High God. Beverly laid back down and fell back into a restful sleep.

The next morning met both Johnathan and Beverly with a cool but sunny day. We're in Chi-town and she wondered if he'd been here before after she saw Johnathan sitting at the table waiting for his order.

She walked up to him and said, "Well fancy meeting you here," laughing out loud. "Oh, good morning Beautiful Lady, please join me for breakfast."

"John what did you order?" Johnathan said, "I ordered, an omelet and a large coffee. I heard this place is famous for their coffee."

"Oh well," Bev said I don't eat eggs, or drink coffee, but you already know that, don't you John?"

"Yes, Bev I do, but they have other choses on the menu and a great selection of teas over there." He was pointing to the table by the wall. Glancing over the breakfast menu, Beverly saw fishcakes and grits southern style. She ordered that and the food was very tasty.

Beverly mentioned to John that she was wondering if the hotel had a gym. She hated to miss her exercise regimen. "That's funny I was thinking the same thing, so I checked on my way here and they not only have a gym, they have an indoor pool also."

"You want to join me later for a swim Bev? "Yes, in about an hour or so, alright? So before returning to their suites, they did some shopping and picked up a few things they didn't have, like a bathing suit and swimming trunks.

On the way to their suites, Johnathan checked with the front desk to ask if any information came in, regarding their flight to Washington.

The desk clerk said, "We're sorry Mr. Sheppard the only information we have is that you may not be able to leave here until Friday or Saturday due to a tornado watch in the surrounding areas. But we have some great sightseeing tours you and Ms. Jensen can catch daily, while you're in town."

"That sounds like a plan and thank you for the message, please keep us posted." "Oh, we will Mr. Sheppard, have a nice day."

Well, I guess we can plan a day swimming then do some sightseeing and shopping, sound good Bev? "Yes, I have to agree with that plan, John." Beverly said, "It sounds wonderful darling just wonderful." In her Marilyn Monroe voice.

Once in her suite, Beverly called Erika and she updated her on the conditions that they were facing in Washington and it sounded bleak. There were piping problems, and the cost was astronomical, even to the point that the project may be scratched entirely.

However, no final decisions had been made yet, the contractors are fully aware that this setback is costly, but they also said that they are doing everything possible to correct this problem and hopefully this project can be completed promptly.

Erika assured Beverly that whatever happens, she wanted

her and Johnathan to use this time as an extended vacation until further notice so enjoy it because it wouldn't cost either of them a dime. "Ms. Jensen, I have to go, I have to take this call, tell Mr. Sheppard I said hello, goodbye now.

"Ms. Brownstone have a blessed day, and please keep us abreast of the procedures, and we won't spend all the companies vacation funds." They both laughed and hung up the phone.

Beverly heard a tap on the door, "Come in John," She knew it was him because he has a special knock, "it's open!!"

"Well I just spoke to Erika, and some major problems in Washington it's delaying the entire project." "What, are you serious Bev?" "Yes, I am John."

"What's happening now, please tell me they are not cancelling this project, are they?" "No John but if things don't get corrected soon that might be a conversation on the table." "Bev, listen, whatever happens we both know that God is in charge."

"There seems to be a lot of negative surprises coming into play, one right behind the other." "I agree John, but we can only wait and see, just be grateful it doesn't affect us. God will reveal His plan in His time, this is what I've learned from my Pastor, and through her teaching and preaching. She has faith that whatever the outcome would be she would say everything would be alright."

"Bev, these rooms are beautiful, aren't they?" Changing the conversation to lighten up the mood. They didn't need to dwell on a problem they couldn't do anything about. "They are nice calming colors." "What color is your room John?" "Come take a look at it yourself, Bev."

She walked with him to his suite. It was huge, and the colors were sage green and brown very manly.

Even the bathroom was a shade of green with light lemon yellow, which were very soft and relaxing. The room came with a large walk-in closet much larger than the one he had in his place, although he had plenty of closet space in his home. He had a bachelor pad if that's what they're still called.

Johnathan wanted to call his sister, but she always spoke much longer than he wanted to hear, so he promised himself, he'd call her tomorrow and update her on everything. Today he was going swimming and enjoying Beverly's company. He looked at Beverly and just in that instant he thought, *"I love this woman."*

Bev let's get out of here while it's still early, that pool is calling our name." they had a full day of enjoyment.

They shopped, they visited two museums, and they took a sailboat ride. Beverly thought to herself, *he sure knows how to treat a lady.* Once they returned to the hotel, they changed for dinner, then went upstairs and sat on the balcony for a while just to have small talk.

Johnathan said, "As much as I'd like to spend some more time with you, I promised myself to call my sister and update her tonight."

"Oh, please don't let me stop you, John, she'll love to hear from you, so, make your call and we'll talk tomorrow and plan another great day." "Sounds good Bev," Johnathan said, "good evening, for now."

Johnathan called his sister, and she updated him on a report about their mother. She was in the hospital again for some chest congestion. "Otherwise she is, the same," JoAnn told him. "How are things going with you?" "Jo we're in Chicago because of the bad weather reports in Arizona." "Johnny, are you kidding me?"

"Where is Beverly? "Oh, she is here also, we are waiting for another flight out but so far the weather has put everything on hold for now. Maybe by the end of the week, we'll be leaving." "Well Johnny, that sounds like an instant vacation to me, with benefits," she laughed.

"Beverly is here, and still on business terms, that's how it is and probably will be for a long time to come." "No, Johnny not if you express how you feel about her, it won't." "Jo as much as I would like to, I don't think Beverly is into me that much. She sees me as her brother or close friend which we are."

"That's all it is between us Jo." "Oh, alright, I'm not going to push this issue but at some point, you need to tell her how you feel about her and you know I'm right."

"Sis, we had a great day today and probably will tomorrow as well. Truly I hope we stay for a few more days so I can reintroduce myself to her as a potential mate. Maybe she'll see me differently."

"Stop dreaming Johnny, tell her. Please promise me you will". "Jo, I can't promise you that." "Johnny, you always say that. When will the time be right?" "I don't know just now, it's not known for sure, Jo."

"Sis, how are you doing?" "Johnny, I'm getting better every day. I have peace of mind, I'm happy and praying for Mom, that's all for right now."

"Johnny, I'm concerned about how Mom's health is

deteriorating. I pray daily that God won't let her suffer too long. She's in God's hands, and He has the final decision, we both know that. If there are any changes in her condition, I'll contact you immediately Johnny."

"I can promise that if anything happens, I'll take the first flight out, wherever I am, Sis, love you, we will talk later, take care of yourself." "Love you back Johnny, bye."

The next morning Beverly woke early to go downstairs to use the hotel gym. She was excited, well maybe not excited, but she was thankful that the hotel had a fully equipped gym. She liked the idea that she could get her morning regimen completed.

After which she grabbed some breakfast since it was complimentary. She didn't bother to knock on Johnathan's door because she heard those ZZZ's through his door.

Beverly was sitting in the dining room and thinking to herself. *Things are not working out as they planned.*

Was she stepping out of bounds taking on this position? Were these occurrences warnings to rethink the plans including relocating? Should she be doubting what she thought was the correct thing to do? She decided to take a walk after she ate and have a talk with God, to ask for clarity.

Wisdom is something she had asked for, and through faith, everything will become clear. She also knew that the enemy always tried putting doubt in our minds, because we are children of the God. Prayer is powerful and Beverly was hoping, or should we say praying that whatever answer she received would be a favorable one.

If it weren't, she would be grateful anyway because she has learned from experience that it's better to be obedient to the Holy Spirit than disobedient and set yourself up for a disaster.

Which leads us to cry out to the Lord for help after we attempted to do things our way instead of waiting and hearing from the Holy Spirit who leads us in the right direction.

Beverly made a mental note to call her Pastor later this evening.

Ms. Brownstone and the Board members were also beginning to disclose their concerns regarding the weather conditions in Washington and what, this storm could do to halt the project plans. Discussions are developing in regard to a different location or alternative state.

These are up in the air presently, but they always need a plan "B" when plan "A" seems to be failing. The Board was concerned with the infrastructure of the area that had been chosen. This was a problem that could ultimately cost thousands of dollars. These decisions were crucial to the future of this company and the people of Washington in hopes of job opportunities.

Erika was again feeling stressed due to the pressure riding on this project. She had put in months of research and planning in the likelihood of impressing the Board that this location would benefit the company and the perspective clients. She expected a positive outcome.

Erika was also hoping that the storm would clear up allowing Beverly and Johnathan to continue their trip to Washington so they could really give a visual account of the damage and get a more accurate report from the contractors.

On top of everything, the Manhattan office was also experiencing major problems. The reports that were given to the investigation department found that there was some serious mismanagement happening with their configurations.

After a hectic disturbing day, Erika went home showered and went straight to bed. Erika usually sat with her family to talk about their day; however, this night she had no interaction with them.

Her husband had noticed that Erika was acting like this more often than usual. He was beginning to voice his concern to her, but she just said, "Honey, I'm tired, I had a challenging day and I just want to sleep." He kissed her and agreed that would be best for her and he would bring her some food.

"Thanks, honey" and laid her head on the pillow and closed her eyes. By the time Evan came back with the food he looked at his wife, and she was in a deep sleep, he didn't want to wake her, so he turned around and took the food back downstairs.

"Daddy is Mommy feeling sick, she didn't say anything to us when she came home?" Evan looked at his three beautiful kids, his two daughters who were watching a movie and his baby boy who was in playpen. "Yes, she is just a little tired that's all!" She needs to rest she'll be fine."

Deep down in his spirit, he felt that it was more than just her being tired. Erika wasn't one to bring her work home with her so unless she was overly stressed about her job, but her excuse was "I'm just tired honey."

Silently Evan prayed she was just tired. In the pit of his stomach, he felt something was bothering his wife. He asked her to take some time off. Erika always ignored his request, telling him that was impossible to do. The job was in a critical state now and she needed to be aware of every aspect of this new project. That was always her answer.

Erika believed that hard work would prove to the Board that she was more than just a C.E.O. So, she had kept abreast of every aspect involving this project. She had worked endlessly, and she could not afford to let anything deter her from the success of this venture.

This was the conversation they had the last time Evan told Erika she needed to slow down, maybe take a day off or take a weekend trip away just to relax for a day or two. Erika refused and walked away from her husband, saying "You don't understand Evan, you really don't, honey!"

As she was walking away, Evan said, "Honey just consider it, please."

Evan asked the girls to set the table and get prepared for dinner. Their nanny had prepared the food for their dinner, and she was feeding his two-year-old toddler. The girls enjoyed eating with their dad but missed their Mother as well.

Usually, she isn't home at the time they usually eat dinner, so this is not strange for them to not have their mom at the table.

Evan had a lucrative computer business. He also worked as an engineer for a transportation company.

After his son was born, he wanted his wife to be a full-time housewife, but that hadn't happened. Evan and Erika met right after college when they were both working in the same building.

After two years of dating, he decided this was the woman he wanted to spend the rest of his life with, so he popped the question, and she accepted. They have been married for seventeen years, and he had never complained about marrying her. She is smart, beautiful, and sexy when she wants to be. They live in a fabulous spacious home, with a full-time nanny for the children. They were well-off and living comfortably.

They have three cars, and the area is secluded from the rest of the noisy world. They both love to entertain friends and family.

Evan has a large family; Erika only has one brother that lives in California. He was always asking them to come out and visit, it's been about three years since they last took a trip out west. Erika's brother has never laid eyes on his nephew due to her work schedule.

He has seen him through web cam, so the baby knows his uncle, Anton. The girls love talking to their uncle too.

Evan considers himself a good husband and father and his main priorities in his life are his God and his family.

Evan asked his wife if she's happy with their marriage and her life she said, "I got my knight and shining armor, my friend, my protector, and my lover." Evan loves when she says that to him, what man wouldn't? Evan always brags about his wife, and some of his male employees say, "Wow, you are blessed. It sounds like your marriage is working beautifully."

Evan would just say, "No man, we're blessed." He tells them once you find your missing rib and know who God is in your life a marriage can survive almost anything." "Believe me, there have been some rough times, but we never give up on each other. Love and faith in GOD can endure whatever the enemy tries to throw our way."

"Hey guys, before you just get any women, make sure she wants to be around for the long haul."

"I've been married for seventeen long years and would never think about leaving or cheating on my wife, it's not even worth it, trust me. I have brothers that went that route and wound up losing everything because they thought the grass was greener on the other side, just to find out the grass was brown in patches." The guys always cracked-up whenever he said that.

Beverly and Johnathan will be checking out of the hotel tomorrow morning heading for Washington to meet with the contractors and executives at another hotel.

"Beverly," Johnathan asked, "Have you contacted your sister and niece yet?" "Yes, I did let them know we were leaving tomorrow." "Thanks for the meal the other day, I enjoyed it and having a man cook is a treat, since I don't have a man to cook for me, so that was really thoughtful of you. Again, thanks so much honey." "John, I didn't know you could cook like that, the food was great." "I enjoyed doing it for you Bev, your great company too."

Johnathan continued saying, "I'll get a chance to do it again sometime soon hopefully." "Johnathan Sheppard, are you flirting with me?" Beverly smiling. He gave her a raised eyebrow look, like no I wouldn't think of doing anything like that, smiling.

Beverly smiled back and shook her head. "Well, I'm going to my suite to finish packing and get some rest before heading out." "One good thing we won't have to get up before daybreak this time." "I agree Bev," Johnathan said. He was thinking to himself, *how he could keep her around a little longer.*

Beverly said, "Oh, I notice that they have a cinema night downstairs. Want to check out what's showing. I'm going to go next door and we can meet up in a few minutes."

Johnathan said, "Alright, great see you in a few minutes, say twenty?" Johnathan had a better idea he wanted to surprise Beverly.

Beverly blew Johnathan a kiss, while in her mind she's saying, *take that anyway you like.*

Once in her suite, she called Anita's number and was glad to hear her voice. "Hi, Sis, what's happening out there in the windy city?" "Girl, it hasn't been a bad layover just an unexpected one. We're on our way to Washington tomorrow or at least the next layover which is Arizona.

How are things there? How's Amber doing, I miss you 'all." "Bev, we're doing good Amber should be coming in shortly."

"I've been busy and guess what I went on a date just the other day. It was a brunch date due to our schedules, but I had a nice time. What have you and my friend Johnathan been up to missy?"

"Stop it, Sis, Johnathan has been a perfect gentleman the whole time we've been here. We've had a good time sightseeing, eating, and shopping."

"All my favorite things to do when you're stuck in a city you were not supposed to be in in the first place. Chi-town is a beautiful place to visit if I must say so myself." The best part is that tonight Mr. Man cooked for me. Sis the food was delicious." "What, girl, you are kidding me?"

"No Sis, for real. The man can cook, for real. Maybe you can hire him when you open your catering business. Just kidding." Beverly said.

Just then Amber said, "Mom. Hi, is that my auntie?" "I sure hope so." "Yes, daughter it is." "Can I speak to her, please?" "Hi, Auntie, how you are, what's up?" "How have you been? How is Chi-town being it cool like in the magazines?" "Slow down Amber, I'm great, and yes it's cool just like in the magazines. Great place to visit. We'll do it one day hopefully, Amber."

"Auntie, I want to ask you a question, I know we spoke about this before, but can I please read your journals?"

"I have a project that's coming up, and I'd love to write

about the three strongest Black women I know. You, Mom and Grandma. We'll be honoring women that have inspired us through our lives. Without a doubt, there is nobody else I can think of but the women in my life. Would you mind if I just read a few of them, Auntie?"

Beverly didn't know how to answer this one, she froze in her thoughts at that moment. Then she said, "I would rather you wait until I come back so I can sort through them." "Auntie, you promise though, right?" Beverly inhaled and exhaled deeply and said. "I promise Amber."

"Oh great, thanks so much Auntie!" "Hope you'll be coming home soon, will you?" "We're not sure yet we haven't reached Washington."

Sweetie, I would love to tell you I'll be home soon but unfortunately, I'm not sure how long this business enterprise is going to take.

But when I get home, I will look through my old journals and see which ones you can use, if any."

"Love you, Auntie." "Love you to Amber." "Listen I have to meet Johnathan in a few minutes, so I'll call when we arrive in Washington.

Stay safe, love you both, later." After Beverly had hung up the phone, she sat on the edge of the bed and went deep into her thoughts regarding those journals.

Those journals that held her painful past, and they are about people that once held power over her, the control they had over her. Beverly learned to thank her Almighty God for His grace and mercy in her life because it could have been worse if the devil had his way.

She glanced at herself in the mirror and said, look, Bev,

those journals are your past, they can't hurt you anymore. You're no longer bound. Stop crying, there's nothing to cry about.

You've made something of yourself. Isn't that what they said you wouldn't do? Look at you, they said you were ugly, but girl you're a beautiful, black successful, educated woman.

Don't waste another tear on those journals. They represent the past, painful or not, it's your past, and this is your future. You're now Ms. C.E.O.

Beverly wiped her eyes and went to freshen herself up before meeting Johnathan, she didn't want to have to explain why she was crying.

Sometimes we need to encourage ourselves. Beverly did her praise dance and stepped out the bathroom rejuvenated.

Beverly put on her little black dress and a royal blue shawl, and she glanced in the mirror again and admired the reflection looking back at her. She walked out the suite and knocked on Johnathan's door. When he opened the door, he smiled from ear to ear. Maybe he was impressed?

"Wow!" "You look... I'm speechless, I mean beautiful, I mean, oh, you know what I mean Bev, but then again you always do lady." "Shall we go?" "Let me grab my jacket." Johnathan escorted Beverly toward the elevators.

As Johnathan and Beverly felt people staring at them, appearing as a well-dressed prestigious couple.

If they only knew they are just two upcoming C.E.O.'s. Beverly enjoyed being with Johnathan, but she was getting comfortable being with him more than she thought she would.

She didn't want to admit it, but it felt good to have

someone take her out for dinner and a show. It had been a long time since she felt special. Johnathan was a gentleman and a handsome one too.

If she was sincerely ready for a relationship, she wondered if Johnathan would ever ask her again, because the way she was feeling at this moment, she'd probably agree to date him. While the ride to the restaurant was interesting and allowing these two-intelligent people to relax they agreed not to discuss the upcoming work-related events.

Beverly asked Johnathan, "how's your mom and sister doing?" His answer surprised her.

Johnathan said, "Bev my mom has been suffering for several years now. We're hoping that she doesn't have to suffer much more.' "I'd rather see her pass away and be at peace than suffer. It might sound mean but who really wants to see their parent suffer?

He continued saying, "while JoAnn has been at her lowest at one time, she is now walking into her destiny. She says she is enjoying her life. She's involved in her church, and she's been drug and alcohol-free for six years. I continue to pray for her strength and that Christ gives her clarity for her new life." I'm proud of my twin sister. Once she accepted Jesus her life became real for her again. For the first time after many years of drug and alcohol abuse, I see my sister at peace with herself, and she loves it. I wish my mom could see her now. God forgives us for all our sins and loves us even in our mess, so I will always praise Him for loving us."

"I know exactly where you're coming from John. My life wasn't always as good as it is now. Lord knows I had my share of hurt, pain, and disappointments. But I learned that when we are His children, His hands surround us even in our mess and I am so grateful that He adopted me into His family. John, we couldn't have asked for a better Father, if we tried." "I agree Bev He's been good to us all."

The driver announced they had arrived. The view was stunning as Beverly stepped out of the town car. This was one of the most celebrated restaurants in Chicago. It's interior displayed pictures of President and First Lady Obama. Oprah, Tyler Perry, Diana Ross, Gladys Knight, Patti LaBelle, Duke Ellington, and many others. Beverly was so impressed she was speechless which doesn't happen too often.

The Paris Club near the River North neighborhood is one of the best eateries around and Beverly loved French dishes. The décor in this place was fabulous, and watercolors made anyone feel cozy. The waiter brought a great choice of wines just to sample. They chose several tasters and picked the two they enjoyed most. Johnathan spoke to the waiter in French and interpreted the menu to Bev in English showing off his French speaking skills. After she made her decision, he ordered their food in French. She was impressed with this man's talents.

This is one of those nights that not many women get to experience. Beverly was thinking to herself; *this is one of the best nights she had in a long time. She could get used to this kind of treatment with someone, one day, hopefully.*

"Bev, hello you alright?" Johnathan asked. "You seem a little distant. "Oh sorry, John just taking it all in.

This is a beautiful place, thanks for bringing me here, I am really enjoying this moment." Johnathan glanced at

Bev and said, "I'm glad you feel that way, I just felt that we deserve the best, I wanted to surprise someone I care about."

At that moment Beverly gave Johnathan a very flirty look. She was having some naughty thoughts that made her smile. They were having a great conversation when the waiter walked up with their orders. Beverly thought to herself, *wow" that's a lot of food, and it looks tantalizing.*

Johnathan touched Beverly hand and said," you should enjoy this dinner. When we get to Washington, we can get some great Mexican cooking. You know those folks love to eat too."

Beverly smiled and agreed with her eyes; she was amazed at all the food they had in front of them. Well, these two C.E.O.'s will remember this night for a long time.

After that great cuisine and the relaxing walk by the river and the sunset, Beverly thanked him for his thoughtfulness, for taking the time out to take her on this fabulous dinner date, and a pleasant evening before they continue their voyage to Washington. Johnathan responded by saying,

"I feel like I'm getting an award or something," laughing, "but it's nice to be appreciated especially by my dear friend. We'll be working together on these projects, so I felt it only correct to treat ourselves, the two people who are the V.I.P.'s for one of the most undeniably advancing companies in the Northeast, wouldn't you agree, Bev?" Beverly smiled and leaned over and kissed Johnathan and said, "How's that for an answer?"

"Hey, girl watch that now, don't get into trouble, or should I say what's done in Chi-town stays in Chi-town?"

Beverly was feeling a little frisky, and she knew it was from a few too many glasses of wine, good food and sexy company. She wanted this man but was afraid of what could happen and what would be the consequence for her flesh becoming weak.

Going back to the hotel the whole time Beverly was thinking, *"How do I handle this Ms. Jensen?" The ride back was quiet neither one said much, but Beverly was sure that John was deep in his feelings by now because she was deep in hers.*

In the elevator going to their suites, Beverly decided to play the shy girl, hoping that would allow her to get to her suite without making an excuse for not following through with what might have followed that kiss. Once on their floor Johnathan being the gentleman that he was walked Beverly to her door and said, "Sweet dreams Beautiful Lady." She turned toward Johnathan and said, "Thanks for everything, good night."

Once inside she sat on the bed and said out loud, "Girl how long has it been since a man held you in his arms, kissed you tenderly and made you feel like he wanted you?"

Beverly knew she'd been putting off a relationship, but it's been a long time since she even had a date, so tonight felt like a date, and she wanted more of them. This wasn't the time. It's never the right time for love or dating, she has a mission to complete, and nothing should interfere with it. Nothing!

Was she too hard on herself? She has to be strong for herself by faith. Her flesh was weak, but her faith is strong. She truly hoped for her sake it was especially tonight.

The next morning Beverly and Johnathan headed to Washington, hopefully with no more glitches. They met in the lobby grabbed some breakfast, and at that point, Johnathan said to Beverly, "Last night was a great evening Bev?" Beverly grinned and said, "Yes, it was John." She wasn't going to make any apologies for what happened last night, and he didn't expect her to.

"Bev," he continued saying before she could finish her sentence, "I know we both are grown, and we are able to control our feelings, but there may come a time that we will be led by our hearts, and that may be how this will have to be handled. That's all I'm going to say about that subject Bev."

Beverly stared into Johnathan's eyes without saying a word for a few seconds, before she said, "John are you ready, shouldn't we be heading to the airport?" "Yes, our bags are at the door, and the car should be here in a few minutes." Beverly grabbed his hand and said, "let's say a prayer and get moving. We have a new challenge ahead of us."

Six hours and twenty minutes later they were landing in Washington. When they arrived, the company had a car waiting for them, and they were whizzed off to the Hyatt hotel and rooms had already been reserved for them.

They were impressed but not surprised since they knew the company would ensure that their executives were comfortable and had nothing to worry about when it came to their accommodations.

The meeting was scheduled for the next day at nine in the morning. This allowed them to relax that evening but when asked did she want to go out for dinner, Beverly politely declined. After which Beverly went directly to her suite and started making calls to let her family know they were safely in Washington. Beverly decided to do some journaling. The one way she could address her feelings was by writing.

The same way she did in her younger years. Now she was not using composition books, Beverly wrote in journals that Amber designed and sold at her school. This reminded Beverly that Amber will be persistent about reading her personal journals, her feelings, and thoughts, and she was sure that she'll have some explaining to do.

Amber is an inquisitive young woman. Beverly decided to cross that bridge when she gets to it.

Johnathan ordered some food and stayed in his suite catching up on some work by answering some issues that had arisen while they'd been gone from the office. He tried contacting Erika but didn't get an answer from the job's number, so he left the message on her answering machine.

Later that evening one of the contractors called Johnathan to rearrange the time for the meeting due to another meeting that took priority. He also mentioned that he was not able to contact Erika and left several messages on her phone. Johnathan knew that Jennifer had taken a few days off, but it was strange that nobody was able to contact Erika.

That was unusual since she always returned his calls and now this made Johnathan a little concerned. He thought he'd call his assistant to find out if they had any information in regard to their boss.

That phone call warranted Johnathan to call Beverly, something he was trying to avoid, at least until tomorrow morning.

"Hi, John," she answered, "What's up?" "Hey, how are you feeling getting some rest, I hope? "Bev, I'm calling because we've attempted to contact Erika to no avail." "That's funny I also tried calling her, and she still hasn't returned any of my calls either." "That's not like her, John."

"The contractor told me the same thing. What do you think we should do?" Johnathan asked. "Maybe you should call her husband, he's your friend correct?" "Yes, he is Bev for many years. Before I do that, I'm waiting for Joseph my assistant to get back to me."

"Well just let me know if you hear anything alright?" "Yes, Bev I will!" Nobody called anyone back that evening, so they decided to wait. The next day they attended the meeting only to receive bad news.

The contractors expressed the troubling circumstances of how the flood left the plot that was chosen for the project. The conditions of the pipes are worse than first expected. The contractors believe that this area had been weakened throughout the years by so many floods.

They also felt that if given more time a better area could be found which would be more beneficial for this project.

Johnathan and Beverly were upset with this report and felt that this should have been researched when the planning was first discussed.

This conversation became a sore spot in the company's plan for advancement in this state. Once Erika is contacted, this decision will be handed over to her and the Board of Directors.

Will it be worth the wait or should we move on to another site? The floods had destroyed most of the area within the perimeters that could have been considered feasible for this project.

As for now, there wasn't any way that Mr. Sheppard or Ms. Jensen were willing to convince their constituents to reconsider this project.

The Board of Directors are in an uproar due to this major setback, and the reality is that it seems inevitable that this plan will have to be re-elevated and put on hold for now.

Meanwhile, Johnathan and Beverly felt that canceling this project completely would be a wiser move. But the final decision would be from the Board and Ms. Brownstone.

Johnathan assured the contractors that another meeting must be scheduled immediately. Another meeting will be arranged within the next week or two and if the contractors can locate another property and the logistics are feasible then maybe the project will be continued.

Therefore, at this time after viewing the damage, the complete project is on hold.

Beverly thanked the contractors for their time and

agreed with Johnathan that she would be in contact with them in a few days as Mr. Sheppard already agreed to do.

At that point, everyone went their separate ways. On the way back to the hotel Johnathan's and Beverly's pager went off, it was Mr. White calling to inform them of some disturbing news. The office had not been able to contact Ms. Brownstone, so they decided to contact her home phone, but to no avail.

However, later that day Jennifer received a call back from Mr. Brownstone that Ms. Jensen and Mr. Sheppard were trying to contact Ms. Brownstone but haven't made any connection.

"Is everything alright, Mr. Brownstone? Hello, Mr. Brownstone are you there? Hello." "Oh yes, I'm sorry Jennifer I guess I can tell you my wife has been hospitalized because she's had a stroke." "Oh, my goodness I'm so sorry to hear that Mr. Brownstone, I'm so sorry." "Yes, we are too Jennifer."

"Let me see if I can get in touch with Mr. White, Mr. Sheppard or Ms. Jensen, they are all out of town." "All right Jennifer, I wasn't thinking, I could have contacted Johnathan, I mean Mr. Sheppard myself. We have been friends for years.

Thank you for your help, I appreciate it." "No, Mr. Brownstone I can do this. Don't worry, please just keep us updated on her condition." "Yes, I will do that goodbye Jennifer."

Evan Brownstone sat momentarily just holding the phone, remembering how many times he begged his wife to quit this job.

She was working too many long hours sometimes six days a week. He would say to her Erika you don't need to work; our kids need you home. We are financially stable my businesses are doing quite well and have been for years.

Erika never wanted to hear what he was asking her; she would always reply "Honey I cannot stop working the company depends on me." Her husband reminded her several times your family needs you too.

Mr. Brownstone can we speak to you please, he heard the doctor say from a distance. "Yes, doctor I'll be right there."

Jennifer immediately contacted Mr. Sheppard and explained what happened to Ms. Brownstone. Johnathan thanked her for quickly relaying the message and asked her to keep them updated also. Johnathan was saddened by this news and silently prayed for her healing. Then he walked over to where Beverly was standing and when she turned and looked at him, she knew something was not right.

Her first thought was, *oh no did something happen to his mom.* "John, what is wrong?"

"Bev remember nobody could reach Erika?" "Yes John, I do, what happened?" "She in the hospital, Bev she's had a stroke!" The thought of this vibrant, hardworking, young woman having a stroke hit her like a brick wall. That thought brought Beverly to tears, literally.

Johnathan consoled her by putting his arm around her allowing her to cry into his shoulder. Once she composed herself, the next conversation was that they needed to get the first flight back to New York.

The main office is putting all projects on hold until further notice. Johnathan contacted the contractors and Mr. Eddie Hernandez who worked out of the Arizona office, informing him of the recent incidents. This meant that this project would have to be delayed now.

Mr. Hernandez told Jonathan and Beverly over the speakerphone that an emergency meeting was being scheduled as they were speaking in the New York office. Some major decisions will be discussed at that time.

All the Board members were also contacted. Beverly was sitting in the chair in Jonathan's suite, and she was having difficulty wrapping her mind around what was happening. Then Johnathan's cell phone rang, and Evan Brownstone was on the other end.

"Evan is that you man? We just heard, I'm sorry man." "Thanks, John but I knew something was not quite right with Erika for a while now. I could not put my finger on it, man. "Now, my wife is in the I.C.U. unable to move." Johnathan said, "What, unable to move from a stroke?"

"Worse man, Erika has slipped into a coma, man this is crazy." "I cannot wrap my head around this. Why my wife?" "Why now?" Johnathan was shocked not knowing how to console his friend or what to say, so he just starting praying trying to comfort his friend. After they prayed, Evan said, "Thanks, man you have always been a good friend. Listen I am going back into her room to hold my wife's hand. Keep us in your prayers, bye man."

Before Johnathan could answer, Evan had hung up the phone. Beverly had overheard the conversation, and when Johnathan turned around, she was just sitting in the chair her mind drifting out in space.

By the end of this stressful day, it was clear that Beverly had to return to New York immediately.

After Johnathan spoke with Mr. White, it was clear that Johnathan would need to stay in Washington a few more days to complete some paperwork and make the necessary changes for legal purposes.

At this point, Johnathan offered to arrange the meetings so he could get back to New York as soon as possible. Beverly said, "John, I guess I should contact the airlines and cancel your seat." "No. Jonathan said," "I asked my assistant to handle all that because I need to concentrate on the details for the next meeting here. Joseph is contacting our lawyers as we speak to draw up the necessary paperwork to close this project."

"Mr. White agrees that we may offer this opportunity to this city at a later date, but as for now, it is off the table. Johnathan realized the process would be delaying his return to New York to deal with this new situation."

"This is such a sad situation, though, John, I'd never even imagined that this would happen to Erika." "How did her family take this news?" It's good she has a nanny for the children."

"That takes some of the pressure off her husband." "I agree, Bev, however, hopefully, she'll recover, and things will get back to normal. A stroke and a coma. "That's a lot for anyone to deal with. I pray for her healing and that the Lord strengthens the family during this time." "Amen."

Mr. White called Johnathan back letting him know that since things are a little upsetting now, Beverly will be considered for Erika's replacement when she returns. Mr. White instructed him not to mention this to Ms. Jensen until the final decision is made, but it was pretty much agreed upon, as far as he was concerned. White assured Johnathan that he would personally contact him later.

Beverly returned to her suite to finish packing. She called the front desk to request car service pick her up and take her to the airport.

Johnathan knocked on her door, and when she opened the door, she smiled at him.

"Come in, as you see I'm ready to leave, so I'm glad you stopped by before I left, but I knew you would. I wanted to thank you for the time we've spent together. I hope when you get back to New York the Board will allow us to continue to work together especially now that things have changed dramatically."

"Bev, I believe that everything will work out, although this is not a happy time for our staff. They will be able to adjust over time, and we must think of the company and our responsibility to our employees and clients.

I hope that doesn't sound too harsh, but we can pray for the Brownstone family and still make sure that the company is running smoothly." "I know John, but this is a sad time for everyone I'm sure. Especially those that worked close with her."

"Well, the car service is probably waiting for me by now, so I'll see you when you get back home, John."

"Alright, let me escort you downstairs. Maybe I'll ride with you to the airport to make sure you get off safely."

Beverly said, "Really, John, I'm a big girl now you don't have to do that! Johnathan's response was, "I know, but I want to Bev, you mean a lot to me, so I want to feel assured that you'll be safe all the time." Beverly leaned over and kissed him on the cheek and this time it ended up on his lips.

She melted inside but tried hard not to show it. Beverly pushed away and said," I've got to leave," and they headed for the elevator. Once downstairs, she checked out and exited the hotel.

Johnathan gestured to the driver to open the trunk. They both got into the car and headed for the airport.

Since the company had arranged all the flight details, Beverly didn't have a long wait before boarding the flight.

Johnathan touched Beverly's hand and held it tight for a minute. Beverly said, "I'll be alright, you know I sleep on planes, I'll wake up and be in New York." Johnathan said, "Call me as soon as you get home promise Bev.

Mr. White will probably be setting up a meeting tomorrow due to the circumstances. Take care of yourself." John, "I will call you as soon as I get settled in, promise." Beverly walked toward the plane and waved bye to her friend.

The flight back to New York was a non-stop one, so she didn't have to change planes. Once home the company provided car service to take her home. When she arrived, she opened her door, but nobody was there. Beverly sunk into her favorite chair and sat quietly for about a half an hour or more until she fell asleep in the chair.

It was Amber who woke her up once she arrived home. Beverly felt exhausted and told Amber she loved her but if she wanted to talk, she'd have to come upstairs after she showered.

Amber said, "I have some phone calls to make, but if you're still up when I finish Auntie, I will. I'm glad you're back home."

The next morning Beverly met Anita and Amber in the kitchen for breakfast and revealed the circumstances that have caused her to return so abruptly from their business trip. While they were talking, the phone rang, and Mr. White was on the other end asking Beverly if she could come into the office and meet with the Board this afternoon.

"This afternoon Beverly asked?" "Yes, Ms. Jensen because the other Board Members were having meetings and won't be able to get here until this afternoon. Would three o'clock be a good time for you, Ms. Jensen?"

"Of course, Mr. White, I'll see you then. Thank you for contacting me and have a good morning." "You too, Ms. Jensen, we'll talk later. Goodbye."

"Wow! that was a short phone call, Bev, it was, wasn't it? Nita." I was just asked to meet with the Board this afternoon. I'm guessing to discuss what changes will have to be incorporated due to Erika's situation. I really feel sorry for her family; they must be deeply concerned about her.

"Well, Erika has been hospitalized she suffered a stroke and now she is in a coma." "OH, MY GOD!" Anita said, "when did this happen?"

"I'm not sure when but we received the call while we were in Arizona. I do believe that these projects became very stressful which could have attributed to this outcome. Johnathan says that her husband was quite concerned about her lately. He said, Mr. Brownstone loves the ground his wife walks on. He knows him personally and said Evan is a good man and a great husband and father. So, he knows he's taking it hard."

But like I told Johnathan we know God is in charge. That's the truth Bev, He has the ultimate plan for her, we'll just keep them in prayer."

"Has anything exciting happened while I was away?" They laughed at that question and said only work and school if you call that exciting. "How was your trip, Auntie?"

Beverly thought about how much she wanted to reveal regarding her recent trip that was more like a getaway with Johnathan.

Even though business was included in the trip, being with Johnathan made this trip more exciting.

"Well, it was very interesting, but the company is about to put those projects on hold due to this recent situation with Erika."

Well, we'll have to catch up later I have several meetings of my own to prepare for, new clients.

Amber is getting ready for her classes. Beverly said, alright then have a blessed day, I'll see you later."

This incident meant that something was about to change and quickly too. Beverly dressed for her meeting with the Board and left the house. Once in the building, she stopped at Carol's office to see if any pending reports needed to be reviewed. She told Carol that after the meeting she would return to discuss how things have been going while she was away.

Carol expressed her sympathy regarding Erika, Jennifer also took the news hard." "I'll try and meet with her once the meeting is over.

Hopefully, she not's worried about being fired or anything like that. I truly don't believe that the Board would allow that to happen."

Beverly walked into Erika's office, and the Board members were waiting for her arrival. The meeting lasted longer than expected they worked late into the evening. So, when Ms. Ellen Teasdale, from the New Jersey office, stated she was getting hungry, the other members agreed with her.

They looked around the office to see if a menu was at the desk, but they didn't find any.

All the kitchens downstairs were closed. Ms. Teasdale wasn't familiar with the area, so she asked Beverly for her suggestions.

Beverly being knowledgeable about the area knew there was a Soul Food restaurant nearby. Everyone ordered, and it wasn't long before the food was delivered.

Ellen Teasdale is a fifty-something-year-old woman married to a top executive in the auto industry. She has two sons who both help run the car business. After they had eaten, they decided to call it a night and finish reviewing the remaining statistics tomorrow.

The Board members had reserved rooms at the Marriott Hotel a few blocks from the office. They expressed their concerns about the company now that Erika has been hospitalized. They asked Beverly, to take the position as the C.E.O for this office. "Beverly, we know you'll do a great job."

Beverly sighed and said, "Thanks for this offer, but what about the Washington deal?" "Mr. White explained that the Washington project is suspended at the present moment. We need you here. You are already familiar with the divisions in this building." "Well if you think you've made the right decision then yes, I'll accept, Beverly continued to be truthful, I was struggling with the idea of having to relocate. God always answers prayers."

Ellen said, "Great we've done enough for tonight." We can continue this tomorrow." They all agreed packed up their belongings and left for the evening. Ellen offered for

Beverly to get a room at the hotel if she was too tired to go home.

Beverly said, "Thanks, but I'd rather go home. I don't live that far away. Everyone get some rest, see you all in the morning." "Oh no, Beverly, we'll be meeting at 9:30 a.m. tomorrow. You don't have to come in early. Actually, you won't be coming in early while you're in this position."

Beverly was a little surprised, but grateful at the same time because that meant that she wouldn't have to leave 40 minutes early due to the heavy traffic in the mornings. *"So, there is an upside to being a C.E.O., after all."* She thought to herself.

Beverly smiled and got on the elevator. Beverly's destination was homebound. She stopped by her office to make sure there wasn't anything that needed her immediate attention then she locked up her files and left the building. She got into her car and drove home.

While driving, she thought out loud to herself, *"Lord, I might not understand what is going on right now. I pray for complete healing for Erika and to strengthen her family at this time, but Lord I'm going to trust you to guide my steps. Give me the wisdom to handle this assignment and patience to believe this is your will for my life."*

"I'm thanking you for this and help me do the best, No Lord let me surpass My Best because this may be a test. I want an A+ when this test is over, In Jesus Mighty Name, Amen."

When she looked up, she realized she was in front of her door. Once inside she went directly to her bedroom, undressed, showered and prayed again, then hit the sack, in that order.

Beverly had been praying for a breakthrough, although she didn't have the faintest idea that the Lord would open such a fantastic opportunity as being offered a C.E.O. position right in her own backyard.

Although it's not a happy time because of the way she obtained this position, getting this position in her home office is an unforeseen blessing. Beverly will continue to pray for Erika's healing every day she walks into her office.

Every day she speaks with her staff, her executives, even the housekeepers and the cooks. Every day she walks into this building praying for Erika's recovery. Beverly dozed off to sleep knowing her prayers would be answered.

The next morning it was pouring rain, but by the afternoon the sun began to shine brightly. Beverly went downstairs to find the house empty, she was hoping Anita would still be home, but nobody was there. So, she followed her daily routine and went to the basement to exercise.

When she finished her workout, she showered and made a green drink before heading out to the next meeting.

Beverly glanced up at the building, all 33 floors and smiled to herself. "Lord, I'm a C.E.O. of this company. Thank you, Lord for this amazing blessing." Beverly couldn't stop thanking her Lord and Savior as she walked into the building. It was close to eight o'clock, and Beverly went into her office to check with her assistant Carol for any updates regarding her divisions.

Carol had been Bev's assistant since she first took the executive manager position sixteen years ago. They actually met in college, and after graduation, Carol moved to Queens, New York. She got married straight out of college and has a set of twin girls that are now in college.

Her husband is a train conductor with the PATH trains. Carol got a job working for one of the smaller companies under this organization's umbrella then her boss Mr. Vance died. That's when she requested to be transferred to this office, and they've been together ever since.

Carol is an excellent, dependable and intelligent Assistant. She informed Beverly that all related information regarding these divisions were sent upstairs for her next meeting. Carol stood in the office door because she needed to ask something. Beverly glanced up and realized that Carol was standing there. "Carol do you want to ask me something?

"Yes, Ms. Jensen, I do. We heard what happened to Ms. Brownstone, and I just wanted to know how she's doing?"

"Carol, I wish I could answer your question, but I really can't at this moment. Hopefully, after this meeting, we may hear something from the hospital or her husband. I'm hoping we're not here as late as we were yesterday. Let's keep her in our prayers."

As Carol was about to leave, Beverly said, "Wait, let's stop by the café since I'm headed upstairs anyway.

You know we love that freshly brewed coffee." Carol agreed, and they walked down the hall to the café. After which, Beverly said, "Have a blessed day Carol, I'll see you later." As she pushed the elevator button.

In Beverly's division, everyone is comfortable speaking to each other on a first name basis, so hearing Ms. Jensen is something she'll have to get used to quickly too. A memo must have come down from corporate informing the staff of protocol.

Beverly exited the elevator then walked up to the C.E.O.'s doors that opened automatically. The team was assembled for today's meeting, and everyone looked fresh and ready to work.

Breakfast from the café had been delivered from downstairs and the same delicious smell of freshly brewed coffee engulfed the office.

Beverly was about to sit alongside Mrs. Teasdale when she pointed at the chair at the head of the table, Erika's seat. This made Beverly a little uncomfortable, but she realized she needed to get comfortable with it. That was her seat now.

The Board began clapping, and congratulations echoed throughout the office. Beverly smiled saying, "Thanks, everyone." After taking a deep breath, Beverly said, "Well, it's time to get down to business."

This day was full of discussions related to pay raises, new work hours along with what seemed like an overload of other subjects that ran through noon. Lunch was ordered from the café downstairs.

The day ended close to seven o'clock. Beverly realized that this new position was going to require a lot of traveling to different business meetings. She wasn't sure she'd be looking forward to extensive traveling any more than she had already been doing for the last couple of years.

According to the team, Beverly would be traveling almost every week to meet with other top executives and managers. Beverly would try and convince them to have as many meetings at this building as possible, instead of her running or flying all over the place.

Mr. George White, from the Albany, New York office had worked for this company for over three decades. Mr. Edward Hernandez from the Arizona office had flown in just for this meeting. Beverly had just met him at their brief meeting.

This Board was willing to work with Ms. Jensen to make this transition a smooth one.

Mrs. Marilyn Gaddy, married to the president of the company's Upstate Division, assured Beverly she would always be available if she needed advice. Mrs. Gaddy stated she would have no problem traveling to this office any time.

The meeting was about to end when the intercom rang, and Erika's assistant Jennifer asked if she could come into the office to set up a conference call from the hospital. Jennifer had put the call on hold for the moment.

Everyone needed to be able to hear this call. Beverly said, "Of course, please connect us and come in if you need to set it up. Thank you, Jennifer."

"Erika's doctor was in the room with her husband." "Hello everyone thanks for accepting this call. Before we start, I sincerely want to thank you for the flowers and cards sent to my family and my wife." There was a pause, he sounded like he was trying to compose himself.

Evan Brownstone cleared his throat and continued talking. "Erika is still in a coma and has not shown any improvement according to her doctors. "We are all praying for her Evan, they all said." "Thanks again everyone."

I'm calling to inform you, Ms. Jensen and the Board Members that is there with you that when or if my wife recovers, I'm not allowing her to return to work. She's been under a lot of stress, "We fully understand your concern and decision" Mr. Brownstone. Evan continued saying, "I want her to recoup and relax fully."

"Mr. Brownstone, Hello, this is Mr. White we completely understand your concern and whatever decision you make." "Well thank you for that, Mr. White." "Oh, excuse me, another doctor just walked in. I have to go, goodbye and thanks again everyone, please keep us in your prayers" "We'll definitely do that, Goodbye."

Mr. Johnathan Sheppard was also on this conference call. He let them know he had spoken to Mr. Brownstone earlier and suggested that he contact Ms. Jensen while she was with the Board and reminded Ms. Jensen that they would talk later. The call was over. Nobody said anything for a few minutes, then Mr. White said," Well maybe we should be making long-term decisions now that we know what we're up against."

After the phone call, Mr. White and Mrs. Gaddy decided to take control of the matter. It was clear that Ms. Brownstone was not returning to this company again. Mrs. Gaddy said, "We have two days to be in this town, and now with this latest development that we'll have to take this seriously, not like we weren't before.

"Since Mr. Brownstone has made his decision, Ms. Jensen

this position is permanently yours. Are we in agreement?" the answer was a unanimous, Yes.

"Ms. Beverly Jensen is the new C.E.O. of this organization." Mr. White went into the other office and made a few phone calls, and before Beverly knew it, they had conference calls with the rest of the Board members.

Arrangements were also being made to make new nameplates, change the name on the glass door and a private phone, the works, for security reasons.

Beverly was thinking to herself, *"Oh my God, this is real."* The team took a break after the intense morning. It was mid-afternoon around 3:30, so it was decided that they would go downstairs to the café after being told how good the food was and everyone could order exactly what they liked.

After lunch, Mr. White and Mr. Hernandez had to leave for another meeting. Before they left it was made clear that they both had spoken with Mrs. Brownstone trying to convince her to take a partner to lighten her heavy workload. She refused always saying she could handle it. We all have held this position, and we never attempted to do it alone.

This building alone has twenty-five divisions; God knows how many employees and managers are here now since she took over.

"Now look at what happened to her, and only God himself knows if she'll ever get better." She has the best doctors in the country, but that's not how we wanted or intended this company to affect a person that works for us. Ms. Jensen, we have to leave, but anytime you need anything, I mean anything please feel free to contact any of us. Also, Mr. Shepperd will be working directly with you, so I'm confident that this transition will go smoothly."

"Thank you, Mr. White and Mr. Hernandez, and I'll remember that. Be safe in your travels." Beverly said. Mrs. Gaddy added her thoughts on this situation also. "Ms. Jensen, you will not be alone in this new endeavor, we have to have another capable person working with you so what happened to Mrs. Brownstone will not happen to you. Please, I don't think the company is responsible for Mrs. Brownstone's condition, she also had other personal issues and an ailing mother that we were aware of.

Mrs. Gaddy continued by saying, "Anyway, Mr. Shepperd will be working with you side by side starting next week. His office will be adjacent to the conference room. He's still out of town as you know, hopefully, he'll return in a few days. We have been in correspondence with him this whole time, and he has accepted the position also. So, the team is confident that this organization will run smoothly with both our most experienced executives running the ship."

"Oh, while we're on the subject Ms. Jensen, you can promote your assistant Carol to the C.E.O.'s executive assistant and Jennifer who was Mrs. Brownstone's assistant can work with both of you for the next three weeks after which time she will be reassigned."

Beverly asked why Jennifer was being relocated. She knew Erika had held this position for at least five years, and Jennifer was the executive assistant before she got the position. It was explained that she lives in Jersey City and there is an office in Jersey with an open assistant position.

"We decided to relocate her this way she'll be closer to home and her children. She won't lose any benefits. We will take care of all her transfer information so don't worry about any of that, she is in full agreement with this transfer Ms. Jensen."

"Are you feeling a little overwhelmed Ms. Jensen?" Mrs. Gaddy asked.

"We're here to ease you into this position and allow you to feel stable. The team executives can handle the minor operational concerns. Which frees you up to deal with the major concerns that go with this title, C.E.O. Well, Ms. Jensen, if you have any questions or concerns now is the time to ask before we leave." said Mrs. Gaddy.

Beverly replied, "At the moment, I believe all is clear, and I'm sure Jennifer can fill in any concerns that may arise." "Jennifer is capable and willing to work with Carol and me until her transfer goes through. We have reviewed all the divisions' reports, and any discrepancies will be discussed with the office managers at our Friday meeting once Mr. Shepperd returns."

Beverly continued saying, "God bless everyone and safe traveling back to your offices and homes." The team stood up shook hands and headed for the elevators.

Beverly sunk down in her new office chair and just stared out the window which looked over much of Westchester County. *"Lord, look where you've brought me from. Nobody would have ever thought I would be sitting in an office building as the C.E.O. and I'm grateful for my blessing and I trust your plan for the future."*

"After so many mistakes you've allowed me to walk into my destiny." Tears streamed down her face, not sad tears, though. If we could see our future, would we believe what we see?

Most of us would not. Beverly's determination to succeed has brought her to this very moment in her life. God's favor on her life has allowed Beverly to crack the glass ceilings. "Thank you, Father."

At that moment Jennifer interrupted her thoughts over the intercom saying, "Ms. Jensen you have a call from Mr. Shepperd, line four can you take it? "Yes, thank you, Jennifer."

"Hi, John how did things go out there?" "Crazy Bev, but I handled it." "Well, John I had no doubt you would handle it that's why they wanted you to stay." "I'm proud of you lady and excited to be working together again." "Ms. C.E.O. what's on the agenda for tomorrow anything pressing?" "No not until Friday when you return, we have an afternoon meeting with the managers."

"Bev, I'm on an early flight Wednesday morning we could meet for dinner and go over the agenda for Friday's meeting. Is that good for you? I'm imagining that beautiful smile and me seeing it every morning or whenever I walk into your office."

"Sounds like a plan John see you then, Oh, and traveling mercies Johnathan."

She was glad he couldn't see her blushing. "I'll call you Bev once I get settled, Bye, for now, "Ms. C.E.O."

"I'm a very busy woman so please try not to call too late, John." "Alright, I'll try goodnight, Oh Bev, have you heard the latest news on Erika

Bev, she's not doing well and truthfully, he's scared, he doesn't think she's not going to make it. I prayed with him, that's all I could do to try and give him some sort of peace of mind."

"It's a tough time for all of us, but I know prayer can change any situation, John."

"We have to be thankful for every day because we just never know, anything can happen from one day to the next," Johnathan said. Beverly was shaking her head in agreement.

"I would like to set up a meeting with Erika's husband to reassure him that we are here for him. Any way we can help I want him to know he can call on us without hesitation." "Bev, I think that's a good idea I'll arrange it once I return."

The light on the phone went off, and Beverly was happy that she had a friend to assist her. It makes things a lot easier when the person working with you is a person you've trusted with major company decisions.

Johnathan keeps himself abreast of the company's policies and regulations, so Beverly was confident that this transition would be achieved.

The day was ending, and she called her assistant Carol to come upstairs so they could go over new details. Carol said, "I can at first, then she said, please, give me a few minutes." Beverly responded, "as soon as you can be fine Carol."

Then Beverly called Jennifer into the office and explained to her that Carol her assistant will be coming upstairs.

There are important details for this transition that needed to be discussed immediately. Jennifer replied, "Yes, Ms. Jensen I understand."

Beverly felt it was important for both assistants to feel comfortable in their new positions. Although Jennifer was leaving, she needed to show Carol all the details regarding her duties as her executive assistant. Beverly was certain that Carol could handle the increased responsibilities. So, this meeting would allow Jennifer to introduce Carol to her new role on the 25th floor.

Beverly realized that the security system allows her to see anyone exiting the elevator, so she asked Jennifer if all the executive offices had the same security screening. Jennifer informed her it was only on the floors where the top executives worked. That would be the next two floors down. Beverly thought to herself, *I've got a lot to learn about this new position.*

Beverly directed Carol to come directly into her office straight ahead. Carol was shocked at first then continued to walk until she reached her Bosses' office. She was quite impressed with the layout.

"Hello Ms. Jensen, WOW! this is amazing, I mean so elaborate." "I know, Beverly said, "But I'm hoping to make some decorating changes more to my liking."

Jennifer said, "Hi Carol, Ms. Jensen that's not a problem

because Ms. Brownstone made changes when she arrived here also. I'll let Carol know who to contact and they will come and make any changes you want immediately."

"Oh, you two know each other already?" "Yes Ms. Jensen, we were in the company's bowling league a year ago," Beverly said, "great that makes this a lot easier. "I've already told Carol about me relocating in a few weeks, and I'll be glad to show her the ropes before I leave."

Jennifer said, "I'm willing to explain all the details for this department that will enable you to make Ms. Jensen's new assignment as smooth as possible.

You'll probably be a lot busier than you were downstairs. Mrs. Brownstone worked late almost every evening. She always seemed to try fitting more than she should have into a day."

"Maybe I shouldn't have said that, but I always worried that she was trying too hard to prove she had it all together, taking on projects that her executive managers were capable of completing. I never understood why she continued to refuse to allow her managers to assist her. It was like she had to prove to herself she could do this job or something. You know what I mean Ms. Jensen?"

"Yes, I do understand, Jennifer. The Board told me they attempted several times to convince her to select a partner to assist her, but she refused. Maybe she didn't realize just how stressful this job can get."

"I felt terrible when I learned she had a stroke and now in a coma, but maybe If she had taken the Boards advice, she might not be in this condition." "Only God knows," Beverly said.

Jennifer goes on by saying, "Ms. Brownstone often complained that her Mother was very ill and that they had a home health aide to assist her Mom. She also had a young baby to care for, along with her two other children."

"Ms. Jensen, please promise that you will take care of yourself and not take on more than is necessary." "Thanks, Jennifer for your concern, but I will not be working alone, Mr. Shepperd will be working with me. I'll definitely keep that in mind."

Carol said, "Once I understand this part of the company, I'll make sure she doesn't Jen."

For the next hour and a half, the ladies sat and discussed some operational procedures, Carol's new duties and responsibilities.

Beverly was about to leave for the day but, instead, decided to stay. She called in orders to the café to deliver their food from downstairs. They worked through the latter part of the day, setting up agendas and preparing reports for the managers.

By the end of the day, they were all mentally exhausted, and everyone closed their offices and headed home. "Good night ladies, "Beverly said, and God's traveling mercies to you both." "Thanks, Ms. Jensen, and God bless you also."

Beverly went downstairs to her office that would soon be given to one of her top managers and checked some messages. She made a few phones calls before leaving the building.

She was able to reach her pastor and told her the good news. Pastor D.E. Wright was excited and said, "See Bev,

God worked it out, and now you won't have to relocate. Glory be to God for His grace and mercy.

How do you feel Bev?"

"Pastor I'm overwhelmed with joy, and I know it's only God's favor that did this although, I'm sad about Erika, she had a stroke and in now in a coma. Can we put her on our prayer list? "Of course, Bev, I have another call, we'll talk later, God bless." "God bless you too Pastor, bye."

Anita was in the kitchen when Beverly arrived home, and she was excited to see her. Beverly said, "Girl, what's up? Wow, that smells great, and I am hungry." "How's everything, Amber home yet sis?" "Slow down lady. First of all, congratulations! God knows you deserve this Ms. C.E.O. YES!!"

"Johnathan updated me on the sad news, all I can say is, But God." Next Amber is at her friend's house they're studying for a test. Please sit down and relax, I know it has been a hectic day for the new C.E.O." "Yes Nita, that's true, it has been ever since I returned."

Beverly headed upstairs and once in her room she laid across the bed and drifted off to sleep. Amber calling her, awoke her, "HI, Auntie!"

"I'm glad you're back, I missed you." "Hi Amber, how's my favorite niece?" "Auntie I'm your only niece," laughing. Beverly thinking to herself, *there's no place like home, it's so true.* "Auntie, you know I prayed that we did not have to relocate, and He answered my prayers". "Honey, God answered all our prayers." "You were to Aunt Bev?

I thought you were excited about relocating?" "Amber if there were no other alternatives then I would have had to be all right with it. Nevertheless, really, I love this community, my home, my job, just where it is."

"So, yes Amber, God does answer prayers. Unfortunately, I would have never wished anything bad on anyone to get it, but it is what it is, and I pray Mrs. Brownstone recovers and is able to go home to her family soon.

On Sunday, Pastor D.E. Wright asked the congregation to keep the Brownstone family in their prayers. Mr. Brownstone had contacted Beverly to ask her church to keep his family in their prayers and it was a heartfelt moment. Later Johnathan contacted Beverly saying, "I'm sorry I missed church service today."

Later that day Amber decided to ask Beverly about her journals. "Auntie Bev, we still need to discuss your journals for my project, although it's not due until the end of the semester. Is it possible I can begin reading them?" Beverly dreaded this moment.

Again, she did not want Amber to think she had something to hide, but once Amber starts reading those journals, there would be questions.

Was she ready to answer those questions? Was she ready

to relive her past? Those were Beverly's questions to herself. "Well, Amber let us wait until I can dig them out and look at them. I'm sure you don't want to read all of them, right?" "Yes, I really do please." Amber left and went to her room.

Now Beverly had to make some concrete decisions regarding her journals. She could open the past and allow her past to help Amber understand why she works so hard to achieve the position she now holds in the workforce and at the same time allowing Amber to complete her term paper on the women that helped shape her life.

Beverly reached under her bed, pulled out a trunk, opened it and started looking at the old pictures. Then, there they were, her journals, twelve journals that held her past. On those pages is her childhood, if that's what you want to call it.

The missing puzzle pieces that have never come together. Missing memories, lost friendships, and unresolved issues, all Beverly's past. Strongholds that kept her hostage in her mind for too many years.

The feelings that attributed to making wrong decisions about men in her life and even how she treated her children but mostly how she felt about herself, which was not good back then. She suffered from abandonment issues, feeling unlovable, low self-esteem, and worthless.... All of this is what is written in these journals.

Beverly sat on her bed opened the first journal she ever wrote in, Beverly loved butterflies so on each page was a butterfly. For her, butterflies represented herself because they started out as ugly little bugs wrapped in a cocoon, not able to move on their own, then after a period of time, their cocoons open and out emerges a beautiful colorful butterfly.

Beverly's young life kept her felling trapped like she was screaming but nobody heard her, unable to move on her own. She recalled times like when she had a gun pointed at her head, or when she got raped twice, or when she was hit so hard, she saw stars, moments that caused her unbearable hurt. She was trapped in relationships; she wasn't strong enough to get out of and those books expressed those feelings.

Beverly started reading, she re-read those words she wrote many years ago. Beverly froze, she could not get past the first page for at least five minutes, It read, *Daddy and I were in the back of the funeral car, and he looked at me and said, "Baby you cannot stay with daddy anymore, you're going to live with Uncle Shorty and Aunt Naomi for a while!" I looked at him and said, "Daddy am I going home with you?" My dad said, "Yes for now, but next month you're going to stay with your uncle."*

Those words had haunted Beverly for most of her life. It was almost like she could his voice.

That man was not her uncle, he was a friend of her dads that would come out years later.

This was the beginning of Beverly's living nightmare, a nightmare that she walked around in for years. Beverly decided that this was her past and if Amber wants to open these closed books of her life, she will allow her to. She reached down pulling all those books out and started walking upstairs to Amber's room.

"Hi Auntie, what's up, are those your journals?" "Yes, Amber here's all of them. These books reflect the feelings of a young girl in a confused state of mind.

Not a crazy girl, just a girl that was hurting for most, if not all of her childhood. A young girl that never felt connected to anyone or anything, and when she did connect it wasn't always a productive one."

"There is one thing I want to explain, it does not matter how your life begins. We all will go through trials and tribulations but what matters is how we deal with them, if we set goals for ourselves then we can create a successful life.

Nobody came to this world equipped with the knowledge of their capability. God has given all His children gifts, talents and when we realize that our gifts and talents are **"OUR PERSONAL SURVIVAL KITS,"** given to glorify Christ to help others then and only then will we blossom.

We should learn who He is and why we were created, then will our lives begin to bring us peace and joy. "Amber, I want you to always remember that you are here at this specific time for a reason, and for a purpose. You may not understand it all now, but as you grow in your walk with Christ, he will begin to reveal your purpose.

I pray that as you read my journals that you will come to realize that even through my pain, disappointments, setbacks and whatever else I experienced, I was determined to prove to the people that doubted me that I was going to succeed and be a blessing to others along this journey called life."

"Auntie, I know that there are things from your past that you never discussed fully. Sometimes in conversations things would be said, tidbits of your past that I picked up on.

Sometimes it was the way you reacted to incidents that happened to mom, or me, or your friends, that you may have expressed I knew your reactions were connected to your past. Auntie, I feel privileged that you are allowing me into your journals, knowing that we usually put our deepest secrets in those kinds of books."

"Amber some are secrets, but I wrote down how I felt or did not feel about what I was going through. I never had time to analyze the situations, I just felt it necessary to prepare myself for the worse. So, I wrote it down in journals or what some people would call diaries."

"I never had time to settle into my surroundings, I never enjoyed childhood like other kids. There are pieces of missing memories I can't put together but hopefully, once you begin reading them, you'll understand what I've told you. Amber don't lose them, and promise not to share......"

"Auntie, I will take care of your journals and only take the information I think I'll be able to use to get my Thesis completed. "Auntie scouts honor, I promise," Beverly said, "Wait a minute, you were never a scout." They both laughed so hard their stomach starting hurting. Thank you for trusting me with your memories."

Before Beverly got up to leave Amber opened the first

book, and the first few lines shocked Amber so much she said, "Auntie is that really what your dad said in a funeral car? Oh, Auntie."

"Amber let's go downstairs before your mom thinks we forgot about that delicious dinner she prepared for us."

Later that evening when Beverly was in her bed, she sat up and thought, *"Thank you, Lord, for the V.O.I.D.s in my life. They have now become my.*

"Victories Over Instant Disappointments."

The ugly caterpillar has evolved!
Into a beautiful butterfly!

Written by Barbra Ju'Don